THE EDGE OF FALLING

THE EDGE OF FALLING

REBECCA SERLE

SIMON & SCHUSTER BFYR

New York   London   Toronto   Sydney   New Delhi

SIMON & SCHUSTER BFYR

An imprint of Simon & Schuster Children's Publishing Division
1230 Avenue of the Americas, New York, NY 10020

This book is a work of fiction. Any references to historical events, real people, or real places are used fictitiously. Other names, characters, places, and events are products of the author's imagination, and any resemblance to actual events or places or persons, living or dead, is entirely coincidental.

For information about special discounts for bulk purchases, please contact
Simon & Schuster Special Sales at 1-866-506-1949
or business@simonandschuster.com.
The Simon & Schuster Speakers Bureau can bring authors to your live event. For more information or to book an event contact the Simon & Schuster Speakers Bureau at 1-866-248-3049 or visit our website at www.simonspeakers.com.
Also available in a hardcover edition
Interior designed by Regina Flath
The text of this book was set in Adobe Garamond Pro.
Manufactured in the United States of America
2 4 6 8 10 9 7 5 3 1
The Library of Congress has cataloged the hardcover edition as follows:
Library of Congress Cataloging-in-Publication Data
Serle, Rebecca.
The edge of falling / Rebecca Serle.
pages cm
Summary: Growing up in privileged Manhattan social circles, Caggie's life appears to be near-perfect but blaming herself for her younger sister's death and being called a hero for supposedly saving a classmate from suicide cause her to withdraw from friends and family until Astor arrives at school, hiding a past at least as dark as her own.
ISBN 978-1-4424-3316-8
[1. Interpersonal relations—Fiction. 2. Death—Fiction. 3. Guilt—Fiction.
4. Dating (Social customs)—Fiction. 5. Family problems—Fiction.
6. New York (N.Y.)—Fiction.] I. Title.
PZ7.S4827Edg 2014
[Fic]—dc23
2013042438
ISBN 978-1-4424-3319-9 (ebook)
ISBN 978-1-5344-8803-8 (paperback reissue)

For Raquel Johnson, Melissa Levick, and Melissa Seligmann

who make all my stories those of friendship

Then perhaps, life only offers the choice of remembering the garden or forgetting it. Either, or: it takes strength to remember, it takes another kind of strength to forget, it takes a hero to do both. People who remember court madness through pain, the pain of the perpetually recurring death of their innocence; people who forget court another kind of madness, the madness of the denial of pain and the hatred of innocence; and the world is mostly divided between madmen who remember and madmen who forget. Heroes are rare.

—*James Baldwin*

BEFORE

"Do you think if I practiced every day I could fly?"

"No," I say, "but you'd probably get taller."

Hayley looks at me with a mixture of annoyance and amusement. She's only eight, but she knows I'm joking. She's like that, wise beyond her years. Able to pick up on the things even the rest of us sometimes can't.

"I'll bet you could," Mom says.

Dad raises his eyebrows, and Peter laughs. "Do you know how much Mom loves you?" Peter asks.

"How much?" Hayley says. She holds her arms out to measure.

"Seems about right."

Dad laughs; Mom kicks Peter under the table.

Hayley goes back to eating her dinner—potatoes and

salmon. Green salad. Peter starts talking about the track meet next week; Dad says he canceled a flight, he'll make it there after all.

Mom and I talk about back-to-school shopping. She asks where I want to go. We'll make a day of it, she says. We'll get our hair done too.

Then Hayley clears her throat, loudly. We all look over. Her eyebrows are knit together, her lips puckered. She looks concerned, focused, but then again, that's kind of her resting state.

"I bet I could," she says. She nods her head down low. If we were strangers, we'd probably think she was done. But then she picks her head up. Her eyes are big, bright. They could lead you home in darkness. "The only thing is, if I got lost, who would find me? None of you know how to fly."

CHAPTER ONE

Most great works of literature have a hero at their core, but this story is an exception. What happened in May doesn't make me a hero; in fact, it makes me the furthest thing from one. What do you call someone who masquerades as a hero? My grandfather had a word for that: phony.

My name is Mcalister Caulfield, I live on the Upper East Side of Manhattan, and this is my story.

Up here, power reigns supreme. Popularity is determined by it. Entrée to clubs and schools and organization boards is determined by it. Even friendship, if you're most of the girls in my soon-to-be-senior class. Power—and of course it doesn't hurt to have model looks, either.

I don't, as my mother puts it, "care enough." I've always been naturally thin, so I have that going for me. But I'm short, too short, and my blond hair doesn't exactly cascade down my back. It's curly at best, frizzy at worst, and rarely thick enough to wear down. While most girls in my junior class spend their Saturdays getting blowouts, I've always opted for the park and a book. That makes me sound clichéd already, but I can promise you this story is more complicated than that. I wish it were just about a poor little rich girl with literary ambitions, but that's not at all the whole truth.

Here's what the gossip papers have been chatting about all summer: In the spring I saved a girl's life. She was hanging by a thread on the terrace of a New York apartment building, and I pulled her to safety.

The headline from the *Post* read: A NEW HERO— LITERARY GOD'S NAMESAKE SAVES A LIFE.

This wasn't the first time people associated me with that character. Is it true? Was my family somehow the inspiration for his story? That would be impossible to tell. And I wouldn't, anyway. Tell, I mean. This is my story. Not his.

Anyway, this girl, the one I supposedly saved—I wasn't friends with her. In fact, I was only at this apartment in the first place because my mom had pressured me into going out that night. Abigail Adams, my classmate and our neighbor, was having a party. My mom said I should go.

My mother didn't used to be like this. Before Hayley, she would have understood why I didn't want to go to Abigail

Adams's. She might have even agreed. But it's like something broke in her, snapped. The thing that made her who she was just stopped functioning. She became generic. She became like every other mother on the Upper East Side of New York City.

When my mother tells the story of what happened last May, she says I ran out the door that night like I was on a mission, like I already knew there was some girl hanging over concrete on that terrace. This could not be further from the truth. I dragged my feet to that party. I dragged my feet one door to the left.

I didn't save her either, but we'll get to that.

Everyone calls me Caggie, by the way, so you should feel free too. My dad came up with the nickname. I've had it since I was a baby. My grandfather ended up marrying a girl from New York named Julie and having two children: my father and uncle. My uncle lives in California and has since before I was born. He's never been married, and he has this gigantic house in Malibu that he's never properly decorated except for the artwork on the wall. No couches, but he has a Renoir painting.

I can't tell you how many times I've asked if I could move in with him.

Then there's my father: married to a fellow Yale grad at twenty-three, an Upper East Side penthouse, a son and a daughter, the same skin-and-bone arms that were bestowed upon him at birth. There used to be more things too, like a Hamptons house and Hayley, but not anymore. Not since January.

"Darling, come here a moment." My mother speaks incredibly quietly for someone who wants your attention as quickly as she does.

"Mm-hmm." I wander into the kitchen and find her all elbows on the counter, flipping through a catalog. She has on a turtleneck, which is only important to note because it's sleeveless. Which is, quite possibly, the most ridiculous garment a person could own. Particularly in the dead of summer. Are you beginning to get a clear picture of my mother here?

She doesn't look up right away when I come in. She's always doing stuff like this: calling you to her and then ignoring you once you get there.

"What's up, Mom?" I ask, hopping up onto a counter stool.

She sighs and slowly turns the page of the catalog she's holding. Then she slides her glasses off her face and folds them down. You could fly to London in the time it takes my mother to begin a conversation.

"I'm considering going to Barneys this afternoon," she says. "Would you like to join me?"

My mother is always considering things, never doing them. She's been this way forever. I have absolutely no idea how she ended up married to my father. She rarely answers a question decisively one way or the other. Do you have to say "I do" in a church? Do they take "I'll consider it"?

"Not really," I say. "I have homework."

"It's summer, darling."

I shrug and play with the end of my T-shirt. "They gave us a reading list."

My mother squints at me. "School starts tomorrow, Mcalister. Don't you think it's a little late to be beginning that?"

"Just finishing up," I say.

My mother knows this isn't true, but she's not going to push it. Just like I'm not going to push her on where Dad has been all summer. I know he doesn't want to be here. I know he doesn't want to be with us—well, with me. But how could we possibly talk about that? There are certain things better left undiscussed, now.

"Is Trevor back?" she asks me.

The question startles me, and I place my hands flat on the marble counter. It's freezing. This house is always freezing. "I don't know," I say. "Maybe."

My mother bobs her head, but she doesn't look up. "So that's that, then?"

I don't answer. No way am I spending the last day of summer talking about Trevor Hanes.

"No to Barneys," I say.

She goes back to flipping through her catalog, and I hop down from the counter and over to the refrigerator. There is nothing in there except for butter and bottled water, though. Our housekeeper usually does the shopping over the weekend, and whenever Peter is home, food is scarce. The thought enters my mind that maybe he's back.

Peter is my brother, and he left last year for college. We're pretty close. Or we were before January. He spent this summer at the beach house with his friend. None of my family besides Peter has been back there, and I have no idea why he'd want to go. If I'm honest with myself, it's been upsetting me. Going to the ocean, cooking in the kitchen, reading in the living room. Splashing around in that pool like nothing happened. An image of Peter lounging on a deck chair flashes in my mind, and my chest fills with rage. I can see the stone tile surrounding the pool, the monogrammed Ralph Lauren towels folded up in rolls. The crisp water bottles with their tops snapped off sweating on the wooden side tables. A lot of details.

That's the thing about these memories: They won't fade.

"Is Peter staying here before he goes back to school?" I ask my mom, still staring at the bottled water and butter.

"Think so. His things are here."

"And the fridge is empty," I mutter.

I hear the catalog fold closed behind me and imagine my mother straightening out, rolling her neck from side to side, the bangles on her arm clanking together. "You sure you don't want to come?" she says.

"I'm sure."

"Suit yourself." My mother is also the kind of woman who says "suit yourself" in a way that makes it very clear that that is the exact opposite of what she means.

She slides out of the room, her stilettos clicking on the ceramic tile. They sound loud, jarring. They echo.

I remember when it wasn't like this. When you couldn't hear heels in this house. When conversation didn't sound like staccato notes on a piano. But that was a while ago now. When there were more people here besides mom and me. When there were still things to talk about that required more than a few words.

As soon as she's gone, I close the fridge and look at the clock: eleven thirty a.m. For some reason, the time reminds me of Trevor. Not that everything doesn't remind me of Trevor lately. Eleven thirty was the time we used to go to brunch on Sundays. He'd show up and ring the doorbell, even though I had said a million times to just come in. "My parents don't care," I used to tell him.

"But I do," he'd say.

He was like that, formal in ways that I didn't think mattered. My parents loved that about him, though. My dad once told me that Trevor was the kind of guy who made it okay not to worry.

He was wrong, though. There was plenty to worry about with Trevor.

After what happened that night at Abigail's in May, I lost Trevor, but I got something too. Something I never really wanted. Recognition. The kind that belongs on a milk carton. I became someone people looked up to. Someone they wanted to be around, hang out with, talk about. I became the most popular girl in our junior class. Because if there's one thing my school, Kensington, loves more than money, it's the feeling of being close to greatness. Like I said: power. They wanted to be close to me. Everyone but Trevor, that is. After last May, Trevor couldn't have gotten far enough away.

My cell phone starts buzzing on the counter.

CLAIRE HOWARD, the screen reads.

Claire is the one person in the universe whose behavior around me hasn't changed this year. I was popular once before, for a heartbeat, when Claire went to Kensington, but then she moved downtown with her parents the summer after sophomore year and that went out the window. She switched schools, which is basically unheard of—no one leaves Kensington. But Claire is nothing if not one of a kind.

Claire is the daughter of Edward Howard, the rock-and-roll photographer. She lives in this gigantic loft in Tribeca with no doors and wears leather year-round. She's always in the front row at fashion shows. She's tall, about five ten to my five two, and she's got these long blond locks that look fake. They are. When you first see Claire, you imagine she's the definition of stuck-up, an Abigail Adams type. But she's the most genuine person I know. She's the kind of girl who would give a homeless guy her purse on the way home from school and not even take anything out first.

She's also a model. She was in the Marc Jacobs show last year. *Vogue* called her "amorphous." We had to google the definition. That article ran the same week the *Post* declared me a hero. "At least we know what that means," Claire said.

"Hey, wild child," Claire chimes.

She's always calling me wild, even though that is about the furthest thing from the truth. She's the wild one. She once spent the night on the balcony of James Franco's Parisian hotel room. She tricked the front desk into giving out his room number. He didn't even come home, but she waited there for him all night. I have no idea what she would have done had he shown up. I'm not sure she did either, but that's the difference between Claire and me. Unknown possibilities excite her.

"Speaking," I say.

"Are you moping at home?" she asks. I imagine her hands stuck on her hips. Raised eyebrows.

"Good morning to you, too."

"It's eleven thirty a.m." The phone gets distant, like she's suddenly far away, and I know she's just put me on speaker. Claire is the queen of multitasking. I think it comes from her dad. I did not inherit that particular trait from my parents. My mother can barely drink water and eat food in the same meal.

"And why do you have to assume I'm moping?" I push on. "I could be having an incredibly productive morning."

"Because I know you," she says, ignoring the last part. "You're probably in the kitchen, still in your pajamas, bemoaning the fact that no one understands you."

"That's pretty specific," I say, gazing down at my Paul Frank monkey pj's. Claire bought them for me for my birthday last year. She wrote "crazy pants" on the label.

"Am I wrong?"

"No," I say, picking up the catalog my mom has abandoned. Saks fall line.

"So what are you up to today?" she asks.

"The usual," I say, studying some patent-leather boots. "Going to Barneys with my mom, meeting up with Abigail for lunch."

"Yuk yuk."

"Come on," I say. "What do you think I'm doing?"

"I think you're going to spend the day locked in your room."

"Locked?"

Claire sighs, and I hear the phone click off speaker. Her voice is clear when it comes through again. "I'm worried about you," she says. "You've barely left your house since June."

"Yeah, well . . ."

"Don't 'yeah, well' me. You had celebrity status for like a millisecond and you didn't even take advantage of it. You know what I would do to be in the *Post*?"

"But you were in *Vogue*," I point out. "Isn't that better?"

She huffs, an *I can't believe I have to explain this to you* noise. "*Vogue* is no Page Six."

"I'm blessed," I deadpan.

"Come downtown," she says. "We can have lunch here. I won't even make you go outside."

"That's a lie."

"Well, we can hang out on the terrace."

"I'll think about it."

She makes a kissing noise, her signature sign-off, and hangs up.

The truth is I'd like to go down to Claire's. Her mom is cool—part old Hollywood, part bohemian hippie—and there are always prints of some new band or famous celebrity lying around on a coffee table. Sometimes her dad pulls us into his studio and asks our opinion on things. The man has photographed the cover of *Vogue* and *Rolling Stone* more times than Annie Leibovitz, and he still wants to know what we think. Their family is like that. They rely on each other. And since I've known Claire for so long, I've become family too.

I haven't really been spending too much time with Claire this summer, though. For one, she was in Europe all of June and half of July, but for another, I really hate lying to her. Not that we talk about that night or anything, but she doesn't know what really happened. It just seemed easier not to tell her, and then it seemed easier to keep not telling her. That's the problem with lying: It's just so damn easy to do.

I head upstairs and decide to change. Our townhouse is three stories, with the kitchen and living room on the first floor, Peter's and my bedrooms on the second, and my parents' room and a gym on the third. My dad's study is off the kitchen. "The worst place to work," he always says. "Food is too distracting." Not that he's ever here. He manages a hedge fund, and he travels a lot, but I know this summer hasn't just been about work. He doesn't want to be around what happened. I've heard that some people manage their grief by compartmentalizing and staying busy. I think my dad has been on a plane every other day since January.

If he's back, Peter isn't currently home. I peek into his room, then head into mine. I pull out some jean shorts and a white gauze top. It's about one hundred degrees outside, and it's crucial to wear as little clothing as possible. I grab my hairbrush from where it's resting on the dresser, careful to keep my eyes trained off the picture of Trevor and me. It's one of us from the winter formal two years ago. He has his arms around me and my head is leaning back on his chest. I think about how it felt that night. How he took me out to the terrace of the Gansevoort, overlooking the Hudson River, placed both hands on the sides of my face, and kissed me.

That was before so many things, though. Before everything, really. Now I don't even know if he's ever going to talk to me again.

I decide to head outside. I shout good-bye to my mom, but the insulation in our house is so impossibly good that she doesn't hear me.

The heat when I get outside is suffocating. It hits you like a fan straight to the face. I turn down Sixty-Fifth, toward Madison. Abigail's building is one over from mine, closer to Park, so this is generally my route of choice.

I have this game I've played since I was first allowed to wander New York alone—which, incidentally, was young.

Probably too young, but that's one of those strange things about growing up here: Your parents tend to forget it's a city and not just your hometown. I tried to enforce some rules with Hayley, but Hayley wasn't one of those kids you had to really fence in. She was smart. She knew the entire alphabet before she was two years old, and she had memorized the Manhattan grid by three years later. She was the kind of kid who had the potential to grow up too fast, because despite her soft brown hair and nose freckles, when she opened her mouth, she could hold her own. People would talk to her like an adult. They treated her like one.

Anyway, the game goes like this: Every time I get to an intersection, I cross whatever street has a walk sign. I only generally play when I have a few free hours, because there are times I end up very far from where I started. I've lived here my whole life, but even I am surprised by where the game sometimes takes me. That's the thing about New York: You can own it, it can belong to you, and you'll still never completely know it.

I've never met a single other person who likes to play besides Trevor, and that could have just been because once upon a time he liked doing things I liked doing.

The light changes at Sixty-Fifth and Fifth and I head downtown, then cross over to Central Park. If you asked me point-blank whether I like living on the Upper East Side,

I'd probably tell you no, but the truth is I really enjoy being this close to the park. I love the anonymity of the park, the fact that, even after spending my entire life on this block of Manhattan, I can still get lost in there. Maybe it's why I play this walking game in the first place: to keep some of that spontaneity new New Yorkers are always going on about. People who come to New York from somewhere else love to say things like "in the time it takes you to cross the street, anything could happen." The thing people forget, though, is that that's true about every town. Not just New York.

The light changes at Forty-Seventh Street and I head farther west, over to Sixth Avenue. I catch a light breeze that fails to pull my top off my back. It's stuck straight on now, and I can feel the beads of sweat gathering at the back of my neck, threatening to drop. You wait all winter for summer in New York, and then it comes and that's miserable too. In the city, anyway. At the beach the summer is exactly as it should be.

My brain goes on autopilot when I play, and without even realizing it I'm down in the Twenties and crossing over to the Hudson River. There is a nice breeze off the water, I'll admit it, and I close my eyes, briefly, and take it in. School starts tomorrow. School with the return of Abigail and Constance and not Claire. I wish she still went there. Last year was miserable without her.

I quit playing the game as soon as I hit the Hudson—it's too hot not to stay on the water—and decide that I'll drop in on Claire after all. I was probably always planning on it, but that's the thing about the walking game: You can't really plan on anything.

Claire lives on the top floor of 166 Duane Street, one of Tribeca's chicest buildings, and the doorman lets me up immediately. His name is Jeff Bridges, like the movie star, and he kind of looks like him too. Speaking of movie stars, Claire's building is crawling with them. SPK used to have a place here, before she split from her husband. I'd see her on the elevator with her kids. She's smaller in real life. Most movie stars are, I've noticed.

I take the elevator to the penthouse and twist my pony-tail up into a bun as the doors open. No matter how air-conditioned their place is, it's always just a little bit too warm in there in the summer and just a little bit too cold in the winter. It's the floor-to-ceiling windows that line the place. They mirror whatever weather is outside.

I figure Claire is probably upstairs on the deck sunbathing, but I call out for her anyway. You never know.

I'm surprised when she answers me. "Kitchen!" she yells.

The Howards' house is pretty much the opposite of ours. While my mother redecorates every eighteen months on the dot, the aesthetic usually vacillates between Italian villa and Parisian glamour. It's not exactly minimal, if you know what I mean.

Claire's apartments have always been totally modern—sleek, sharp lines. They redecorate, but when they do it's always subtle, the kind of thing you don't notice until months later, when you're admiring a lamp or picture or whatever and you realize it wasn't always there. The loft has barely any doors, and it's all white, interspersed very sparingly with color—shots of fuchsia and green and midnight blue. And of course there are massive photographs everywhere. Their entire apartment looks a little bit like an art gallery, right down to the fact that there is barely even anywhere to sit.

I make my way into the kitchen—a massive stainless-steel industrial affair—and find her standing in front of the refrigerator in a see-through gray sundress that is probably actually lingerie.

"I thought you weren't coming over," she says, spinning around and giving me a wide smile.

I smile back. "No you didn't."

Claire is so beautiful that it could literally take your breath away. I mean that. When she walked in the Karen Millen show last fall, I think more than a few people had to remember to exhale. She's all legs and arms and hair—the kind that glides down her back. Fake, yes. But still beautiful. When we're out together, even if it's just on the street or something, nearly every person we pass turns around and looks at her. They think she's famous, possibly that she's even someone else, that they've seen her on TV or in movies. She once did a guest stint on *The Vampire Diaries*, but that's all she's done besides modeling so far. She says she's too all over the place to commit to a career, but I think she secretly wants to be an actress, and I could totally see her in California. Maybe she doesn't think she could cut it; I'm not sure. It's hard to think of Claire having any insecurities.

I shrug. "I felt like walking."

"You *walked* here?" Despite her five-ten frame Claire never wears anything but heels. Walking more than a block without a driver following her is pretty much her definition of hell.

"You know I do that," I say, lifting some more strands of damp hair off my neck and securing them back in my bun.

"It's like a hundred degrees out, though," she says.

"Not like," I say. "Actually."

She opens the fridge, takes out an Evian water, and slides it across the counter to me. I twist off the top and down half the bottle in one swig.

"Where are your parents?" I ask, wiping the back of my hand across my mouth.

"Europe," she says. "Maybe Italy?" She starts munching on a green apple, then holds it out to me. I shake my head.

"You weren't invited?" I ask.

It's very unusual for Claire's parents to travel without her.

When she was away June and July, she was with them. They've never cared about pulling her out of school. She once went to school in Prague for a whole month. Her father travels all the time for shoots, but if her mom goes, generally Claire does too.

"Of course I was *invited*," she says, setting the apple down. "I just didn't want to go." She looks at me, her eyebrows raised.

"Still?" I ask.

Claire nods, her eyes wide.

Claire has been hooking up with the front man of Death for Grass, an up-and-coming indie rock band. She's been seeing him since the Fourth of July, which in Claire time is like decades, and I figured this week they would be calling it quits. Claire isn't exactly known for her long-term relationships. She's got a six-week attention span, even when traveling. You could set your watch to it, and right now, the timer is about to go off.

"He's incredible," she says. "He made me a picnic last night."

"Where?" I ask.

"Prospect Park," she says, her eyes glazing over.

"You went to Brooklyn?"

She snaps back to attention. "I think I'm in love," she says.

I feel my stomach clench and release. Claire says this a lot, and most of the time she just forgets after a bit, like the emotion was a symptom of a passing cold or something. But once, one glaring time, it totally shook up her universe. And, by extension, mine. David Crew, sophomore year. They dated from September through February, and when they broke up, it was hellish. She dropped ten pounds in two weeks. Claire doesn't have ten pounds to lose.

I take another sip of water. "That sounds serious."

She comes closer, in a rush, and leans over the marble counter toward me. "He's just remarkable. You know what he said to me? He said he wanted to tell me things he has only ever written down."

"I'm not sure that's an improvement from his initial opener," I say. "When he was quoting Coldplay lyrics to you?"

She raises her eyebrows at me and then nods in understanding. Claire and I have this thing we do when she's on first dates. She leaves her phone on, and I listen on the other end. It's supposed to be so that if he's boring, or she's having a terrible time, I can come down and interrupt it. I've only ever done it once, though. A guy suggested they karaoke, and if there is one thing Claire really, really hates, it's singing onstage. I crashed and told him her cat was in the hospital. Claire doesn't have a cat, but it got her out of there.

Most of the time, if he doesn't sound like a serial killer, I let her suffer her way through.

"What does that even mean, though?" I say, squinting at her.

She rolls her eyes. "Like he wants to tell me things he's only put in songs or in poems but he's never spoken out *loud*."

"Okay . . ."

"Stop being so cynical."

"I'm just surprised," I say. "You're talking a little out of character." Claire usually sees dating as a pastime, not something to get invested in. Love to her is like a holiday—fun while it lasts. It took her like a year to understand why I'd make Trevor my boyfriend. She loves love, but commitment? Not really. Like I said, she can barely commit to spending the entire evening with one dude.

Claire tucks some hair behind her ear. "I don't know, I really don't. It's like everything I believed about relationships before this was completely false. Like I was just operating from this place that didn't *know* yet. Do you know what I mean?"

"Yes," I say, keeping my eyes down. I bite my lip, but the words come out anyway: "That's how I felt with Trevor."

Claire's voice gets quiet. "Right. Have you heard from him yet?"

I shake my head.

"I'm sure you will. I think he just thought you needed some space." She plays with a hangnail, her eyes fixed on her fingertips.

She keeps saying that: "He thought you needed space." But he could have asked me. He could have done anything except just leave. I don't know how to say that to Claire, though. Because she doesn't have all the information. There are some things you cannot share with friends. Even best ones. Some secrets that are kinder just to keep.

"Should we go up to the roof?"

Claire squeals. "Really?" She pulls down the strap of her sundress to show me her bare shoulder. "Do you see this?"

"See what?" I ask, leaning forward.

"Exactly," she says, shaking her head. "No tan line. Travesty."

"We can rectify," I say. "Do you have a sun hat?"

I've forgotten mine, and I'm sure I've already gotten singed on the way down. No matter what I do, how much sunscreen I wear, my skin always opts to burn, not tan.

"Sure," she says.

I follow her out of the kitchen and into her room, where she has full-length mirrors on one side and windows on the other. It's impossible to avoid seeing yourself in here, and when I look, I see that I'm right: My cheeks are the color of tomatoes. She tosses me a floppy straw hat with a huge brim and puts on a bathing suit top. "Want one?" she asks, holding up a blue polka-dot piece of nylon.

"No, thanks. I think I've gotten enough color today."

She purses her lips in the mirror, like she's blowing it a kiss, and then we're walking back out through the living room and over to the kitchen. There is a spiral staircase that leads directly from the apartment to the Howards' own private roof deck.

"Oh, I forgot to tell you," she says, pausing on the railing. "I got some inside info."

"Yeah?"

She looks down at me and smiles. "Kristen is coming back to the city."

It takes me a moment to register what she's said, but when I do, it doesn't matter that the apartment is ten degrees too warm. Inside, I feel frozen.

"Where did you hear that?" I ask, trying to keep my voice level.

Claire shrugs and continues to climb. "Can't remember. Around? Pretty cool, right? Guess she's doing better."

I swallow. Hard. "Yeah, guess so."

Claire stops again and peers at me. "How come you don't seem happy? That means she's okay, you know. You did a good thing." She jabs me in the ribs, but I barely feel it. All I can feel is that cold seeping out into my veins, like my heart has sprung a leak.

I follow her all the way up the stairs. Claire's rooftop is impressive. I'm reminded every time I'm up here. You can see over the whole Hudson, and they have lounge chairs and outdoor furniture set up, a big barbecue in the corner. A bar and a bunch of potted trees—something that sort of looks like a palm but isn't.

We've had a few really good parties up here. And by parties I mean me, Claire, Trevor, Peter, and Claire's friends, most of them older models or photographers or DJs, sitting around drinking champagne and watching the sun set—or come up.

We set up our towels on two matching recliners, and Claire grabs Evian waters from the outdoor refrigerator. The sun is beating down hard, but I can't feel it. Even as my back begins to sweat, the beads gathering on my collarbone, my hairline, the bridge of my nose, I still feel cold.

You did a good thing.

If I could go back to that night in May, I'd do things very differently. I'd never end up on that rooftop with Kristen. I'd never save her. I wouldn't have to.

But even stories with the biggest impact, perhaps particularly these, don't have the power to be rewritten. If if if if . . . would everything be different? It doesn't matter now. What's done is done.

Let's keep going.

CHAPTER TWO

I first met Kristen Jenkins in the third grade. She had just moved from Minnesota, and she was this tiny girl with strawberry-blond hair and the thinnest arms I had ever seen. She was quiet and shy, and I remember thinking she was too fragile to withstand Manhattan. I may not like it all the time, but at least I was born here. I know how to deal with this city.

She generally kept to herself, and she continued to when we got to Kensington. I didn't really know her. Not well, anyway. I knew the standard things, the things that everyone knew: only child, lives on Lexington Avenue, father is a lawyer. But I didn't know *her*. Not until May, anyway. That was the night I learned that the things we often don't ask about—ignore, walk by—those can be the most deadly of all.

After the May incident, as people started referring to it, she left town. Immediately, actually. It was the end-of-the-year party, but we still had a few finals to take the next week. She didn't show. Abigail said that they mailed her the exams. There was talk of her returning to Minnesota, but one girl, I think it was Constance Dunlop, said she saw the forwarding address. It was some hospital in Maine.

I try not to think about that now. There is no way to change what happened. It just did. And she didn't end up dead, anyway.

I'm just going to go ahead and tell you up front the truth about May. No one knows this. Not Claire and not Trevor. Not Peter, not my parents. Not even Abigail Adams herself. Only Kristen and I.

Look, technically I did save her. But she wouldn't have needed to be saved if I hadn't been up there in the first place. If I hadn't been standing on that ledge. I'm sorry, you probably don't want to hear that, but things haven't been so easy since January. I thought maybe I could make them easier. Maybe I could just not be around anymore. How could I tell people that, though? How could I tell people that the reason I was up on that roof was that I no longer wanted to be alive? And I can't tell them now, either. Claire would freak out and my mom would probably put me in a mental hospital. They don't need to be burdened with this. They've been burdened enough already.

I told you this story wasn't about a hero. Do you see what I mean now?

Claire is in her closet trying to figure out what to wear to meet Band Guy, the new love of her life, when I decide to go home.

"If I don't see you before tomorrow, have a great first day!" she calls from the floor, two opposing wedges in her right and left hands.

"You too," I say. I don't think I've ever told Claire just how much I miss her at school. I know she'd feel bad about it if she knew how miserable I actually am there without her. I know Kensington. I've lived at Sixty-Fifth and Madison my whole life. But it doesn't mean I fit in there. That's the thing about the places we come from—they probably say the least about who we really are than anything.

I decide to take the subway uptown. I need some time to think, and I can never think as well in cabs as I can on the subway. For one, I get carsick, and for another, I always feel self-conscious in cabs. I feel like I should talk to the driver or something. That's what one-on-one interaction forces. I prefer being underground. It's comforting, in an odd way. Too many people crammed into this moving metal space. You feel really small down there, insignificant. You'd think that would be a

z

bad thing, but it's not. It's one of the best feelings in the world.

I consider getting off at Fifty-Seventh Street and going to find my mom at Barneys—it would make her so happy—but I just don't feel like seeing Abigail or Constance or any of the other girls who could be there the day before school starts. So instead I head home. It's well into the afternoon and still so hot I welcome the subzero environment of our apartment.

When I get back, I see a suitcase in the foyer. Blue Tumi, *PSC* stitched on the front.

"Peter?" I call.

I hear some movement on the stairs, and then Peter is standing on the landing, a smile on his freckled face. "Hey, kid. Miss me?"

"Yes," I say. "Despite myself, of course."

"Of course." He wrinkles his nose at me, and then he's tearing down the steps, grabbing me into a big hug.

"Okay, okay," I say after a moment, although I'm just now realizing how much I've missed him this summer. It's the first summer we've spent apart in our entire lives. Camp was never really our thing; we always just went to the beach. I can smell the sand and ocean air on him. It makes me long for things—some that have gone and others that I left. None that I know how to get back.

"How was the summer?" I ask.

He pulls back and makes a face at me. "I saw you three weeks ago, Caggs."

"Yeah, well . . ." I glance down at his suitcase. "You packing or unpacking?"

"Both," he says. "But my flight leaves tomorrow. You want to hang tonight?"

I eye him. "Felicia okay with that?"

Felicia is Peter's girlfriend. They've been together for about two years and have been trying to make it work long-distance this past year. She's at Columbia, here in the city, but Peter is off in Los Angeles at USC. It doesn't seem to get him down, though. Not much does. Peter is the kind of guy who can spin just about anything into a positive.

"I'll see her later. I need some time with my baby sister." He slings an arm over my shoulder, and we step around his suitcase. "How's Claire?" he asks.

"She's good. In love."

"Love?" Peter drops his arm and gets in front of me. "Our Claire?"

"Since when is she 'our Claire'?" I say, trying to jostle past him.

Peter doesn't let it slide. "Since forever, Caggs. How long has she been your best friend?"

I shrug. I'm not surprised, exactly, that Peter cares about Claire's romantic life. I think he's always carried a torch for her. He's just never copped to it before.

"Speaking of being someone's . . ." He puts his arm back around me as we continue toward the kitchen. "Have you seen Trevor?"

Peter thinks this thing with Trevor is a break. He doesn't get it. All at once I'm angry again. The same anger that's licked at me all of July and August like a white-hot flame: Peter decided to spend the summer there when he should have been here.

"No," I say. "We haven't exactly been in touch."

He gives my shoulder a squeeze. "I think it's temporary," he says.

"Yeah, well, when he broke up with me he didn't really give me a timeline."

"Come on, Caggs. You two were together for like a year and a half. That's about a decade in teenage years. You don't just throw that away."

I punch him lightly and he laughs. "Okay, okay," he says.

I move to take a cup down from the kitchen cabinet. I stand over the sink and let the water run before I fill the glass. My parents have some fancy purifier attached to the faucet, but I don't bother to turn it on. With everything that's happened in my life, I doubt some chlorine is really going to be the thing to do me in.

The thing is, though, Trevor did throw it away. It was obvious for months, possibly even since the start of spring, if I think about it. Things just kept getting worse and worse.

I kept getting worse and worse. And I wanted to be the girl he remembered, the girl who ate ice cream with him on the High Line and snuck champagne into movie theaters and ran around Washington Square Park in the summer in the rain. If not for me then definitely for him. But I couldn't. After Hayley I just didn't work the same way. I could have done all those things, but we wouldn't have enjoyed them. I wouldn't have really been there.

I didn't blame him when he broke up with me. It was my fault. I knew it was coming. I had probably known for months. He didn't understand that I couldn't be honest with him. What he didn't know was that he wouldn't have wanted that. He didn't want my honesty. Because I could have told him everything—how I really felt about Hayley, what was happening with my family—but it wouldn't have made things better. It would have made things far, far worse. He would have felt responsible, somehow, for everything. That's the kind of guy Trevor is. He thinks he can somehow affect the course of my life just by existing. But that's not how it works. If it did, well, things would be different.

"I don't even know where he's been," I tell Peter, leaning against the sink and taking a long swig of water. "I don't even know if he's coming back."

"He's . . ." Peter crosses his arms. "Of course he's coming back."

"Yeah? How can you be so sure?"

Peter takes a pear out of a basket on the counter and flicks it in the air. "I saw him today."

My chest feels like it's an elastic band that's just been snapped. I swallow. "Where?"

"On the street by his place. Seventy-Second, right?"

I nod. "Did he say anything?"

"Not really," he says. "But I didn't ask."

Peter is the kind of guy who would run into Oprah and comment on the weather. He doesn't push people, or seek out answers. It's one of the things I love most about him: You never feel like he's going to corner you. But right now I'm annoyed with him for taking everything so lightly. Some things in life require anger and sadness and pain. When Peter acts so carefree, I can't help but feel like he's lying.

"I guess I'll see him at school—"

"Look, Caggs," he says. "I'm not going to tell you what to do."

"Good," I snap.

"*But*," he continues, "you should cut the guy some slack. It's been a tough year."

"Really? I had no idea." I cross my arms and look at him.

"I'm just trying to tell you it's okay to move forward," he says.

My annoyance at him blooms into full-on anger. "Just

because I don't feel like spending the summer frolicking around her grave site doesn't mean I'm not moving on," I shoot back.

As soon as the words are out, I feel horrible. It's a familiar feeling, that acid in my stomach—like some small balloon of poison that's been punctured.

Peter looks at me, unblinking. "Is that what you think?"

I shake my head. "No," I say. "It's not."

"Good, because I wasn't frolicking."

"Whatever," I mumble. "I know you love it out there."

"Caggie, listen to me." Peter's voice is stern. "I went out there to pack up the house. Mom can't do it, and I doubt Dad would either. Who else is going to sort through that stuff?"

"They're selling it?" I ask stupidly.

Peter nods. "Yes." He runs a hand through his hair. "I don't blame you, but try to think a little bit before you just assume things."

I had no idea my parents were selling the house. I guess I should have figured they would, but I kind of saw it as sitting there, untouched. Which is why it was so disturbing to me that Peter would want to spend the summer out there—cooking there, sleeping there. I wanted, if I'm honest, for everything to stay the same. Maybe if we didn't move anything, if we kept it exactly as it was—the overturned chair, the back door slightly ajar—then she would find her way home.

But that's not the way it is. She didn't run away.

"Sorry," I mumble.

Peter nods. "Fair enough."

"Is anyone interested yet?"

Peter bites into the pear. "I mean, we're talking prime beachfront, Caggs. It'll go quickly."

"Right."

He sets the fruit down and comes over to the sink. "Hey, it's okay. It was actually not so bad being out there. I found some of her old paintings." He runs a hand over his forehead and smiles. "She's was such a crazy little artist."

"A good one," I say.

Hayley loved to paint. There is this room off her bedroom that our mother always thought was a closet but that was actually more the size of a study. I helped Hayley turn it into an art studio. We bought everything: oil paints, big canvases, brushes, smocks. I've never seen anyone as happy in my life as she was when we brought it all home.

She'd spend hours in there. Her big thing was birds. Huge canvases of them. She was a total amateur ornithologist; she knew every species. We'd be watching a movie and there would be a bird noise, like a background sound, and she'd be able to tell you exactly what species it was, where it came from, what color its wings were. That was the kind of kid she was. She really cared about the things she cared about.

In May, after the incident, I found a bunch of supplies still in Hayley's studio. There were her paintings, all wrapped in bubble paper, but then some unused stuff too. Unopened oil paints, a bowl still coated in her favorite shade of fuchsia. The one she had mixed up herself.

I'm still not sure what to do with it all. I can't quite bring myself to throw it out. It was her life dream to be a painter. Every time I try to clean up in there, I imagine her standing in the doorway, her hands on her hips. *What do you think you're doing?* she'd say. *I'm not finished with that.*

Peter nods. "I miss her too, Caggs. But we shouldn't pretend like we can close the door on that. It isn't something to lock up."

"Yeah." I slide past him. "Look, I'm going to get some stuff organized for tomorrow. But we could grab dinner later if you wanted to."

"Definos?"

"You know it."

He puts his hand up and I tap it with my palm. "Call Felicia," I tell him on my way out.

He rolls his eyes but I can see a smile on his lips. "Okay, boss."

I wander back to my room thinking about Trevor. A million thoughts flash through my mind at once. He's back. Why hasn't he called? Why would he call? Is he mad at me? Where did he go? And then: Does he want to get back together?

No, he doesn't want to get back together. Why would he? He hasn't so much as sent me an e-mail to let me know he's alive.

But when I walk into my room, I don't have to think about where he is, or whether he's going to call, because he's standing right there. He's facing the window in my bedroom, and he doesn't immediately turn around. I just stand in my doorway, looking at the back of him—the curve of his neck, the shape of his arms. Arms that wrapped around me. I used to think that if he held me as tight as he could it would keep everything in place. It would keep my mind from running away, from remembering. I was wrong.

I clear my throat. "Hi," I say.

He spins around, and when he does, I'm reminded of the first time I saw him. It was freshman year, the first day at Kensington, and I wasn't expecting to see too many foreign faces. Most of the kids I already knew. They were kids I had gone to Wheatley with, grown up with. They were my neighbors. But then I spotted this boy standing by the admissions office, leaning against the wall by the door. He was flipping through a course catalog, and he had this light brown hair and tanned skin and the bluest eyes I had ever seen. They seemed to soften when he looked at me, like they went from being fixed sapphires to tiny pools of water with a single glance.

We didn't become friends then. We didn't even speak at all. But I'll never forget the way he looked at me. Like he was melting.

"Hey, Caggs." His face is soft, and I notice his hair has grown longer this summer. It's always wavy, kind of floppy in the front, but it sweeps down below his ears now. He runs a hand through, lifting it up off his forehead.

"How did you get in?" I ask. My voice cracks on the last word.

"You always said I shouldn't knock," he says. He smiles, but it's just slight.

He moves closer to me, and my heart starts hammering. I forgot how attractive he is. How even now, with so much terrible history between us, a huge part of me just wants to kiss him. To run my hands through his hair and feel his breath against my ear.

Trevor pauses in the middle of my room. "How was your summer?" he asks.

"How was my summer?"

He drops his eyes to the carpet. "Yeah, I mean . . ."

"Trevor, I haven't spoken to you in two months."

"I just thought . . ." He stops, starts again: "I just wanted to see how you were."

I cross my arms. "I'm fine."

"I can see that." He smiles, like he's trying it on, seeing if it will catch. When my lips don't move, his face falls.

"Are you going to tell me where you've been?" I ask.

His forehead pinches together. "In LA," he says. "I assumed you knew." Trevor has grandparents out in LA, and he goes every summer to visit them. But it's usually just for a week or two.

"How would I know?"

He squints and looks at me, opens his mouth. But then he shakes his head and doesn't say anything.

"You didn't even call," I say.

"I didn't think you wanted to hear from me." He pauses, crosses his arms. "Was I wrong?"

I inhale. I want to tell him that yes, of course he was wrong. All I wanted all summer was a phone call from him, to hear his voice or see his name in my inbox, but I can't admit that. He broke up with me. He's the one who ended things. All there is left to do now is prove I've moved on.

"Is that all?" I ask. "Is that what you came here to say?"

"Caggs . . ."

I turn away from him, toward my door, because all of a sudden I'm afraid I'm going to cry. And if I start, I have a feeling I'm not going to be able to stop. It's better to keep that stuff low. Way down at the core, like where they bury radioactive waste.

"I have a lot to do before tomorrow," I whisper, my back still turned.

He walks to where I'm standing until I can feel him behind me. I close my eyes as he reaches out and touches my back, right below the shoulder blades. "I'll see you," he says.

Then he's moving past me, out the door. I watch his frame disappear down the hallway, and listen for his feet on the stairs. I can't hear them, though. You can't hear anything in this house, not even when it's right next to you.

CHAPTER THREE

There are two types of students at Kensington. The ones who have parents who went there, and the ones who don't. Meaning the ones who are new to the Kensington Way. Kensington is the oldest private preparatory academy in New York. It dates back to 1842, and used to be an all-boys school until like the seventies. My father went there. His father before him.

Abigail Adams's father went there. Constance Dunlop's parents went there. Kensington: Educating the Future of Manhattan, One Intolerable Child at a Time.

Kensington is located right across from the Metropolitan Museum of Art on Museum Mile. Even though it's no more than fifteen blocks from most of my fellow students' homes, some of them actually take cars in the morning. The mornings at that place are completely ridiculous—a bunch of black town cars pouring out sixteen-year-olds in skirts, ties, and knee-high socks. Sounds like a television show, right? It would be if they'd ever let cameras inside. Abigail tried to get a reality show off the ground last year, but the board voted that no video cameras would be allowed on school premises. My mother cast the deciding vote. She's been on the board since I was born, maybe even before. My mother may be a tiny woman, but she has a lot of power. So does my dad. And it has nothing to do with their jobs. People have a strange fascination with my family that lets us get away with things.

Personally, I like to walk. I'm not a morning person, not by a long-shot, but I just can't stomach being dropped off by a guy in a chauffeur hat at seven forty-five a.m. It would give the people around me too much pleasure. Trevor walks too, and last year I used to meet him on Fifth at Seventy-Second Street. He lives on the West Side and crosses the park at Sixty-Sixth. He'd have a cappuccino for me, and we'd take our time with the thirteen blocks up. We'd even hold hands sometimes, if we felt like it. Those mornings were my favorite part of the day. Just the two of us, wandering the streets of New York. Together.

I race downstairs, glancing at the clock: seven thirty, damn it. If I walk, I'll be late. Peter is seated at the counter inhaling cereal, and my mother is staring at the espresso maker like if she looks at it from the right angle, it will start working on its own.

"Morning," I say.

Peter cocks his head up at me; my mother doesn't move.

"What time is your flight?" I ask Peter, nudging my mom out of the way and setting the coffee machine in motion.

"Four," he says. "Wanna take me?"

"I'm not out until three." I raise my eyebrows at him. He knows that. Once upon a time he went to Kensington, too.

"Ah, right. But it's senior year. You can skip, right?"

At this my mother snaps back to attention. "Absolutely not," she says. "Albert will take you, and Caggie will remain in school." She nods to herself, pulling down a mug. Albert didn't used to exist, but now Dad is gone all the time, and when he's here he's not exactly in the mood to play chauffeur. At least not to me. Mom doesn't drive, and isn't a huge fan of taxis.

"Well, there you go," I say to Peter. I grab a muffin off the counter and he pulls me into a quick hug. "Will you be back soon?" I ask his shoulder.

"Next month," he says, releasing me. "Maybe earlier. Felicia's got some kind of big match." Felicia is a tennis player. She got a scholarship to Columbia for it too.

My head falls a little. After Trevor left yesterday, Peter and I spent the night in our family room, eating greasy takeout and watching old karate movies. We were only interrupted when Claire called to talk about the latest date with Band Guy. I put her on speaker and Peter kept rolling his eyes. I hadn't laughed that much all summer. I hadn't really laughed at all, honestly. Having Peter around makes me feel okay again, like maybe things won't be this way forever. I don't want him to go.

Peter reads me. "Soon, kid," he says.

I grab my backpack and head out the door. It isn't even shut completely behind me when I hear her voice. The shrill alert of none other than my neighbor Abigail Adams.

Good morning to me.

"Mcalister!" she sings out.

Abigail is short, and she's got this pin-curled red hair that she usually wears back with a ribbon or headband. Her uniform is tailored to be just a little bit shorter than accepted, but not so much that she's breaking dress code, and today she has on a purple tie with the Kensington insignia. She has about a hundred custom Kensington ties. Passed down for generations. They are probably the same ones her grandfather wore.

"Hey, Abbey." She hates when anyone calls her Abbey, so naturally that's what I do.

Abigail huffs. "Do you want a ride?"

I flip my wrist over to glance at my watch: 7:37. I'll never make it in time.

"Sure, that would be great," I say with a smile.

Abigail eyes me, and then motions with her hand. I duck into the waiting town car after her.

She slings her book bag on the seat next to us—this season's Miu Miu tote, the same one that's in my mom's closet—and unsnaps a water bottle from the minifridge. She hands me one.

"Thanks," I say.

"So," she says, turning to me. "I'll bet you're excited to see Kristen, right? Have you spoken to her at all this summer? Such an amazing thing that happened that night at my house." She emphasizes the "my." Then she takes a swig of water. "It was really so lucky we were both there, wasn't it?"

"Yeah," I say. "Sure."

"I can't imagine being an outsider here," she prattles on. "I bet it was always really difficult for her. You know, when I heard about"—she lowers her voice, like the driver is going to do something with this information—"*that forwarding address*, the first thing I thought was I'm glad she's getting the help she needs." She presses her hand to her chest. "I mean, I felt horrible, but at least she was somewhere they were taking care of her, you know?"

"I doubt she was in a mental hospital," I say, and as I do I can feel the half muffin I inhaled rolling around in my stomach. At least I think she wasn't. I hope she wasn't. She would have told her parents the truth. She would have told someone. The thought of that, of how fast news spreads at Kensington, makes my blood run cold.

Abigail seems put off by this. "Caggie, it's okay, you know. You saved her, but it doesn't mean she didn't also have to save herself."

Abigail looks beyond pleased with that maxim, and I wonder when she thought it up and how long she's been waiting to say it.

She keeps talking as we drive. About responsibility, and dogs, and some neighborhood-watch program she's thinking of starting. I just nod and smile in a noncommittal way, hoping that we don't hit any red lights. Finally, the car pulls up to school. I immediately open the door and launch myself out.

Even I have to admit Kensington's campus is beautiful. It's got that old New York look. Stone columns, redbrick buildings. It's regal and welcoming and totally forbidding all at once. It's not a terrible place to go to school, if you want to know the truth. I just wish Claire was here and that Trevor and I were, well, anything. Friends, even.

Claire and I were in the fifth grade when her parents relocated from LA. She was this gorgeous Malibu transplant who already had a handle on the New York scene. I was a fifth-generation New Yorker who had never even been photographed for New York Social Diary. We were an unlikely pair, but we fit perfectly.

Abigail follows me inside. "It's just like Mrs. Thompson sooo doesn't get my schedule. How are you supposed to do piano and clarinet and still have time for chorus? I'm trying to make Juilliard here, not give myself a hernia."

"Yeah," I say, already mentally checking out of the conversation. I have English first period, with Mr. Tenner. I haven't had him since sophomore year, but he's been my favorite teacher ever since. He's one of those cool teachers, but he doesn't try too hard. I think if you had asked him at sixteen what he wanted to do, he would have said teaching.

"Caggie, assembly?" Abigail gives me a withering glance.

"Right."

Every other day at Kensington there is High Assembly. They try to make it this super-formal thing where we have to sing the school song and pledge allegiance and all this business, but really most students sleep through the thing. They take attendance, though, so you have to be there and check in with your advisor, even if you don't pay attention.

There are two girls in my grade, Gidget and Bartley, who aren't too bad. I spot them when I step inside the hall. If I miss a class and need the homework assignment or something, I usually ask one of them. I can't say they've replaced Claire, but at least there is someone to talk to who isn't Abigail Adams.

They're the kind of girls who won't immediately say something bad about you the second you leave the room, and at Kensington that's a pretty valuable commodity.

I make my way over to them and sit down next to Bartley. Of the two she's probably a bit prettier—her hair is a little longer and it looks more naturally blond than Gidget's does. "Hey, guys," I say. "How was your summer?" Despite liking them all right, I haven't actually seen them once since June.

"It was great. We were at the beach!" Gidget nudges Bartley and she winces. "I mean, we . . ."

"It's fine," I say, catching on. "Glad you guys had fun."

"Of course," they both say together.

They were nice about Hayley, too. They didn't harass me the way my other classmates did. Constantly asking if there was anything they could do, following me home from school to make sure I was "okay."

Abigail walks up to the podium and launches into a speech about how this is going to be the best year yet. About how Kensington has been "leading the world frontier on excellence" for the last hundred years and how we owe it to our fathers and forefathers to uphold their tradition. Lots of applause. A few slow claps.

I make a point of not looking around for Trevor. He's a pretty dedicated student and always on time to these things, so I know he's there. I just sit back and let Abigail's shrill turn into a drone. Kensington isn't looking promising this year, and I haven't even had my first class yet.

The single thing I miss the most about Claire being at school is how every day felt . . . unknown. Like there was the possibility for something totally different to happen. The time we ditched and snuck into Madison Square Garden when they were setting up for a Prince show. Claire knew one of the security guards. We ended up spending eighteen hours in there, on the side of the stage.

Then there was the time we dumped food coloring in the school pool, and when the swim team showed up for practice, the water was a deep purple, like Gatorade.

I couldn't dump food coloring into the Kensington pool on my own. If I tried, which I wouldn't, I'd probably just dye my hands and then get in troubling for staining my uniform.

When I get to first period, Tripp Remington and Daniel Jeffreys are already there, sitting on the tops of their desks. They never say more than ten words to me, which is totally fine in my book.

Tripp used to date Abigail. Or does. They've been pretty on and off for most of the last two years. He comes from a journalist dynasty. His father's company owns a media empire. Every magazine you read? They publish it. He and

Daniel have been slouching their way through school with me since the first grade.

"How was your summer?" Tripp asks.

"Fine," I say, a little surprised they're showing any interest. I shouldn't be. People have been treating me differently this year. "I kind of just hung out in the city. You guys?"

I slide into a desk near the back left-hand corner. Tripp shakes his blond locks out of his eyes and swivels to face me. There are rumors he dyes it. His hair, I mean. I wouldn't be surprised. It looks almost identical to Claire's, and she says she's seen him at her salon downtown.

"Went to Brazil." Tripp socks Daniel in the arm. "Boys' trip."

"Right," I say. "Sounds fun."

"Epic."

Students start to file in around us and take their seats. I assume we are done with this little conversation, but Tripp leans in closer. "I just want to say," he says, his voice dropping, "that I think what you did last spring was really cool." He nods at Daniel, then turns back to me. "I mean, not many people can say that, you know? That they saved someone's life." He straightens up, like he's proud of himself. "If you ever want to like talk about it, or whatever, I'm here." He winks at me, then socks Daniel in the arm again, and the two of them drop into their seats.

Talk about it. Right.

Sure, I'd love to tell you the story of last May. Of how Abigail Adams threw a "Welcome Summer" party at her apartment. About how I went up to her penthouse roof to get some fresh air and spotted that the safety gate on the ledge, the one the window washers use, had been undone. About how I saw Kristen standing there on the six-inch platform, the city swaying below her. About how I selflessly stepped over that railing and took her hand in mine and asked her not to do this, to climb back over with me. About how I was just about to get through to her when she slipped. About how she screamed and everyone came running.

They piled onto that roof deck like sunbathers on the one sunlit strip of beach at high noon. They watched her dangle twelve floors above the concrete jungle, our fingers still locked. They saw me haul her up and both of us collapse on the floor, tucked back safely on the other side of the gate.

But you already know that's just one version of this story. And I'm getting tired of telling it.

"I'll keep that in mind," I mumble.

People start hustling in, including Trevor. We took Mr. Tenner's English together sophomore year, and Trevor liked it even more than I did, so I should have assumed he'd be here. He hangs in the doorway for a second and catches my eye. He smiles—that soft, sweet, heart-melting smile—and slides into the only available desk: two rows over, the same seat as mine.

Hey, he mouths and holds up his hands like *who would have thought?*

I give him a small smile and face front, but my heart is racing. It's ridiculous that after two years, Trevor can still light my pulse.

It's always been this way, though. He came to Kensington from The Anderson School on the Upper West Side, and from the first day freshman year there was just something about him, something that made me want to be close to him. A lot of girls felt it too. He was the new hot commodity on campus, the boy with the soft brown hair and blue eyes. He was sensitive and kind, and when you spoke to him, about anything, he'd listen, like you were the only person in the room. The only person in the world, really. Most girls in our grade wanted to feel that from him, and I was the one who got to.

We didn't become friends until sophomore year, but once we started hanging out, it was instant. It felt like I had known him forever. I recognized him and he recognized me. It didn't take very long after that for us to be a couple. I remember the exact day, the exact moment. We were sitting in my room with Hayley. She wanted to paint us, and she had her whole station set up—her canvas board, easel, watercolors. "Hold still," she said. "Don't move so I can do it properly." That was when he did it. We were sitting side by side, and he just reached across, ran his thumb over my cheek, and kissed me.

Hayley put up a fuss. She said that we were disobeying her orders, we were *moving*, but when she gave me the painting a few weeks later, it was of us just like that: his hand on my face, his lips brushing mine.

I try not to think about that now, though. Because now we're not together anymore. We can't go back.

Mr. Tenner asks us to take out our syllabuses. I see we're reading Virginia Woolf and *Nine Stories*, J. D. Salinger's short-story collection, this year. I happen to be a huge Salinger fan. I own multiple copies of all his books: *Franny and Zooey. Raise High the Roof Beam, Carpenters.* When we used to go up to the Berkshires, I'd make my parents stop at every book-store to try to scour for first editions. I've gotten some off the Internet, too. I couldn't admit this to anyone, because it would seem too obvious, like it meant something different from what it does, but he's my favorite writer by far. It's the way he so clearly identifies humanity. It's crisp and sharp. Like iceberg lettuce, or a knife. You don't know whether you want to bite into it or use it to cut through something.

Mr. Tenner is counting down the books, explaining what we're going to attempt to finish before December break, when Kristen walks in. I'm immediately struck by how tiny she is.

She's always been small, even shorter than me, and she's got ice-white skin that's almost translucent—ghostlike, even. But she looks even smaller than I remember. She holds her hand up to Mr. Tenner. "Sorry I'm late," she whispers.

The room erupts into deafening silence—the kind that's filled to the brim with glances and raised eyebrows and restrained gossip. Everyone is looking between her and me and Mr. Tenner, who motions for Kristen to take a seat at the empty desk in the back. He doesn't pause for more than a moment before he keeps on lecturing.

Kristen weaves her way left. *Please don't look at me,* I silently pray. *Not in front of everyone.* Seeing her now makes it all real. The things I pushed aside over the summer. The whispers I ignored and buried down right there with the truth. What if she actually spent the summer getting treatment? The thought of it makes me feel ill, makes the room spin—like a globe flicked into motion.

She takes her seat, and we plod through class. I pull out my notebook and begin scribbling. I'm not even writing coherent sentences, but anything to look busy. I can feel Trevor's gaze on me, heavy like concrete, and I can feel the pull of Kristen—what I'd say to her if I could.

I spend class in a state of hyperconsciousness. My upper back feels hot from tension, but I don't pick my head up from my notebook. I'm afraid of whose eyes I might meet.

There are chimes between classes at Kensington, no bells, and when the tinkling sound goes off, everyone grabs their book bags. The Kristen drama seems to have evaporated over the last fifty minutes, and now students are way more interested in their bone-dry cappuccinos than whether or not the disturbed girl and the one who saved her are going to embrace each other after a long summer's absence.

I slide my book bag over my shoulder and make my way toward the door. I only stop when I feel a hand on my back. "Caggie?"

I turn around to see Kristen, students knocking past her, Trevor included. He half waves as he leaves, but I'm so distracted by contact with Kristen that I don't respond.

"Hi." I swallow.

She smiles. Relief floods my body like warm water. "Could I talk to you for a minute?" she asks.

"Sure." I shift my backpack from one shoulder to the other. I peel a hangnail off. Up close, Kristen looks good. Tiny, but well. Her skin is even a little darker, like she spent time in the sun this summer. I hope that's true.

She waits until the students have barreled out. A few turn back to look at us, but there are only five minutes between classes at Kensington, so no one can really afford to wait. When the last student has left, she turns to me. My heart beats frantically, like it's trying to run away from this conversation.

"How was your summer?" I ask. I try to keep my voice casual, but I can feel my pulse in my neck.

"It was good," she says. "Calm." My mind jumps—calm like . . . *medicated*? She smiles, and her warm, brown eyes seem to slow my racing blood. "Don't worry," she says. "I just went home to Minnesota. I saw my old friends, stayed with my grandparents. It was exactly what I needed."

I exhale. "Right," I say. "Good. I didn't really think . . ." I trail off, look at my shoes.

"How about you?" she asks.

I screw my face up into what I hope is a smile. "Good! You know, busy. Well, mellow, I guess. I didn't really . . . I mean . . ." I sigh. "It was fine."

She shakes her head. "I meant to call you, but I wasn't sure . . ."

I look up and meet her gaze. "Same," I say.

"You know, it's all right. I'm not . . ." Her brown eyes are fierce. "I'm not going to say anything."

I look away and shuffle my feet a few times back and forth in lieu of words. This kindness isn't what I expected from her. I should say thank you, but I can't bring myself to get the words out. I also don't know if she means it. She may know my darkest secret, but I barely know her.

"I'm glad you're okay," I say instead.

She takes it and nods. "So I'll see you around, then?"

Kristen looks up at me, her eyes wide, and for a moment I see her on Abigail's rooftop, hanging from my fingers, her face wild with terror. "Definitely," I say.

And then I duck past her, just as the chimes start to go off again. Class is beginning.

Lunch at Kensington is an interesting affair. No one really eats in the cafeteria. For one, most girls in my class have been on a diet since they were about ten, so lunch either consists of gossip or celery. For another, one of the perks of Kensington is that you're allowed off campus at lunch. It's always been this way. It's meant to foster "community appreciation," which means Kensington is somehow under the delusion that its students use the freedom of their lunch hour to check out the new Imperial Age exhibit at the Metropolitan Museum of Art. Mostly what happens is that they go to the park and make out. Claire and I used to do that, minus the making out part, no matter what Tripp says. Trevor always had some school-related project to attend to at lunch—an extra AP class, prep for a debate, etc.—so at lunch it was just me and Claire.

We'd pick up sandwiches from Caffe Grazie on Eighty-Fourth and go eat them on a bench in the park. Even in the winter. If it was really raining, we'd duck into Island on Ninety-Second and sit with coffee. Besides mornings with

Trevor, it was my favorite part of the day, and now, staring at our school's sandwich stand, I miss Claire more than I have in a year and a half.

"Come with us!" I turn around to find Abigail and her girl squad a few paces over, handbags on their shoulders, primed for escape.

"Oh," I say, "I don't know, I . . ." I gesture toward the sandwich stand, which never has a line. Today is no exception. With New York at your fingertips, who would go for a turkey and rye at Kensington?

Abigail marches toward me, hooks her arm through mine, and starts dragging me to the double doors that lead into the courtyard and out of school. "We know you and Trevor have broken up and Claire hasn't been here in a year." Abigail looks at me pointedly. "And we think you should start spending more time with us this year."

Constance Dunlop and Samantha Bennett nod emphatically.

"Thanks," I say. "That's sweet of you."

They bookend me so there is no way to get out as we head straight into the park. Sure enough, we don't stop to pick up food. It's hot out, but not as sweltering as yesterday. Even with Abigail's arm linked through mine, it's nice to be in here. A slight breeze curls around a bend and picks up my hair, cooling the back of my neck.

"Here," Abigail directs.

She lets go of me, and Constance produces a blanket, which she and Samantha sit down on. Abigail follows and so do I, so we're all making a little circle. I half expect them to pull out a Ouija board.

"I heard you talked to Kristen after class today," Samantha blurts out. She leans way forward, sticks her chin in her hands. "Tell us everything."

They're getting filled up on gossip. Obviously. I brought lunch.

"There's nothing to tell," I say. "She just wanted to know how my summer went."

Constance and Abigail exchange a look. "Did she say how that mental place was?" Samantha giggles. "I heard they had to strap her down so she wouldn't run away."

"She wasn't in a hospital," I say. My voice gets quiet, and the three of them lean in closer. Abigail's eyebrows travel up her forehead like they're trying to reach her hairline.

"Yes she was. Constance saw her forwarding address," Samantha says.

Constance has busied herself with rummaging through her Chanel purse.

"Well, she wasn't," I say. "She was just with her grandparents." I lean back on my hands.

"Yeah, but come on," Samantha presses. "You don't just try to kill yourself and then give it up the next minute. That's not how it works."

"Really? How *does* it work?" Constance says. Samantha clocks her in the side, and both girls tumble over, laughing. Only Abigail stays upright.

"Did she say anything else?" she asks me.

I close my eyes into a spotlight of sun. "Not really."

"Okay." Abigail is silent for a moment. "It's just, she tried to *kill herself.*"

I open my eyes and find her looking at me. Constance and Samantha are lost in another conversation. Something about the way Abigail is leaning forward, squinting, like she's trying to read something off my face, makes my heartbeat quicken.

"That was a rumor," I say.

"She was on the ledge of our roof terrace," Abigail says. "What do you think she was trying to do up there? Enjoy the view?"

I thread some grass through my fingers and pull. "It's over. It's a new year. I think we should just move on. Leave her alone."

"Can you imagine if you didn't get to her in time?" Abigail says, shaking her head. "I can't even think about it." She shudders, like she's suddenly freezing. In reality the cloud cover has lifted and the sun is beating down, full force. "I guess you know what you're going to write your college essay on," she says, winking at me.

That's the thing that's always really stunned me about these girls. Their ability to go from dead serious to ridiculous in no more than a second. How can you switch gears that quickly?

"So you were at the beach this summer?" I ask, trying to steer the conversation away from Kristen.

"Yep," she says, suddenly animated. "You know Tripp came out for a full week? He didn't even stay with his parents, just with us." At this Samantha and Constance jump back in, exclaiming how Tripp showed up with flowers and insisted on making Abigail breakfast in bed, even though they had a full-time summer chef out there. Abigail leans back on her hands. "I think he's the one," she says after a moment.

I gawk. "The one?"

She smiles her patronizing smile. It says, *Someday, dear, you'll know what I'm talking about.* "I think we'll get engaged," she says.

Constance and Samantha start squealing. They sound like tiny animals in the wild.

"You're seventeen," I say, slowly, like maybe she's forgotten.

"Oh, not *now*," she says, waving her hand around. "I just mean *someday*. He'll start working for his father, you know,

REBECCA SERLE

and it would just *make sense* . . ." She starts rambling about Park Avenue real estate and summers in Bridgehampton and I feel that pang again, the pang of missing Claire and Trevor. The only two people in my life who ever validated my suspicion that this world is a total and complete farce.

I remember when I could have said the same things about Trevor. Not the marriage part, not beach houses in Bridgehampton, but things that made sense. Things like going to the University of Iowa for their writing program, starting our own literary journal. We'd always argue about whether or not we wanted to end up back in New York. He did. He said he wanted to live on the Upper West Side, where he was from. I couldn't imagine living here, having just the park to separate me from Kensington and everything that comes along with life here, but Trevor said that the park might as well be the Atlantic Ocean and that Kensington wouldn't matter once we left. "That's the thing about New York," Trevor used to tell me. "You can make it whatever you want it to be."

I knew he was right, but there was always something so alluring about the idea of moving somewhere where it would be just the two of us, where no one knew us. We could read and write and have a tiny cottage and a vegetable garden. It all sounds so ridiculous now, but at one time it was the only thing I wanted—to have him in my life forever.

"We should get back," Constance says.

Samantha yanks the blanket out from under and the four of us march back down Fifth Avenue toward Kensington. I'm starving, but there's no time to get anything now. I think I have an old granola bar stashed somewhere in my locker. Do they go bad? Probably not.

As we're passing through the gates, back inside, I spot Trevor. He's seated on a bench in the courtyard, his arms crossed, looking toward the sidewalk like he's waiting for someone. When he sees me, he straightens up. He lifts his hand and waves, but I don't mirror him. I can't bring myself to wave back. He smiles with just the corners of his mouth. His smile seems to say, *This is pretty sad, huh? Where we've ended up?* I want to agree, to shake my head, run to him, laugh at how out of hand everything has gotten, but he ended things. When you're the dumpee, you don't have those kinds of privileges. He keeps holding my gaze until I look away.

"Ex stalking much?" It's Abigail, in my ear like a mosquito.

"What?" I say.

"Trevor obviously still has a thing for you. He's like a pining puppy."

"No he's not," I say, trying to swat her away.

"Yes he is!" Abigail squeals out.

"Trust me," I say. "If Trevor still has feelings for me, they're just pity. We're done." And then I walk off toward history, making a mental note that, no matter how lonely I get this year, I will not, under any circumstances, submit myself to another lunch with Abigail Adams & Co. Some things are just not worth it.

CHAPTER FOUR

"Hey, wait up." I turn around to see Trevor jogging behind me.

It's three o'clock, and this year I'm determined not to stay at school a moment more than necessary. I used to run track and the school paper—I was the first junior to ever make editor—but I gave that up in January. It just seemed so trivial. Everything did. And the stories we ran were pointless. Taste tests on Diet Coke vs. Coke Zero? I couldn't take it.

"Trevor," I start.

He holds up his hand. "Wait, I just want to talk to you." He sticks his hands on his knees, panting. Despite his tall frame, Trevor has never been very athletic. He used to come watch my track practices and tell me he was tired just being there.

"And say what?" I'm trying hard to remain composed.

His face slackens, smooths out, and I can't help but run my eyes over his cheeks, his ears, the freckle on his face. I think about how many times I've kissed that exact spot. When someone breaks up with you they should take their memories with them. It shouldn't be possible to remember someone when they're no longer there.

"I heard you and Kristen today," he says.

My breath catches. "Heard us what?"

He looks at me. That look he has that I know means *stop bullshitting.* "What isn't she going to tell?"

I take a deep breath but don't automatically say anything. I hate lying to him; that was part of the problem. He could sense it, I know he could. But I also can't tell him. Just like I can't tell Claire. It wouldn't be fair. To them or anyone else. I just pray Kristen meant what she said. It would be so easy for Trevor to ask her . . . and she has no reason to protect me.

"I thought you left," I say lamely.

Trevor shakes his head. "Come on, Caggs. I heard her. What was she talking about?"

"Nothing," I say, turning around and walking. "Just forget about it."

Trevor follows. "I know something happened. Why won't you tell me?"

"It isn't important," I say.

"Like hell it isn't." Trevor grabs my arm. It's hard, and I'm surprised. Trevor never gets annoyed or raises his voice. "Stop shutting me out," he says.

"I didn't shut you out," I say. I'm still moving forward, fast, trying to get away, but Trevor won't let me.

"Yes you did," he says. "After January you wouldn't even look at me." His fingers are still on my bicep. "Come on, Caggs, it's *me*. You can talk to me."

I'm suddenly filled with anger. The force of it sends me whirling around to look at him, and I shake his hand off. "Why are you doing this?" I ask. "Are you forgetting that *you* broke up with *me*?"

He shakes his head. "You think that's what I wanted?"

"Pretty sure, yes," I say. "Because it's what you did."

Trevor throws his hands up, the way he does when he's watching a soccer game that's going particularly badly. "You forced me to. After your sister died—"

"Don't do that," I say. "Don't bring her into it."

Trevor softens. He reaches for me. His hand grazes my arm. "I was just going to say you let me be there, in the beginning . . ." His voice trails off. "It got worse, not better."

I close my eyes. His touch, his words, are overwhelming. Having him this close makes me feel more than I have in months. I'm not sure I like it. Feeling too much is dangerous.

It makes me want things I can no longer have. It's what led me up to that rooftop. "She didn't come back," I say. "How could it have gotten better?" I shake my head, take my arm back from his grasp.

"All I ever wanted was to be there for you," he says, his gaze dropping to the ground beneath us. "I didn't know how to do that. I left, and I should have stayed. I should have forced you to—" His voice breaks. Trevor has never been shy about his emotions. He cried watching *The Notebook*. I think it was his suggestion to download it too.

I know my resolve has cracked somewhere in the course of this conversation. I need to get out of here before I break open completely. I cut him off. "Are we done?"

He looks at me, his blue eyes pierced, but when I turn back around and start walking, he doesn't follow.

I walk all the way home. I know he isn't behind me, I can sense it, but I want to turn around anyway. I have to fight the urge all the way to my front door.

When I get inside, my mother is contorted on a mat in the living room, her Pilates instructor standing over her. "Claire called," she says, her leg making circles in the air.

I'm surprised, because usually she doesn't remember messages. These days she doesn't answer the phone too often, and Claire always calls on my cell, anyway.

"When?" I ask.

Her Pilates instructor, some guy named Leaf or Tree or River, gives me a pointed look.

"No problem," I conclude for myself. "I'll call her back."

I leave them and head into the kitchen. I'm struck by how much I miss Peter, just knowing he's not here. It's weird: He was gone all summer, but having him back yesterday made me get used to his being around. It's amazing how easy it is to fall back into old habits, how just a few hours is enough to catapult you backward, at least emotionally. But emotions don't matter. They aren't fact. Peter is at school, where he lives now. Things aren't the same. I push Trevor out of my head as I reach for the phone.

"Caggs," Claire says when she picks up.

"Yes, Claire Bear. You rang?" I can hear her plodding around her bedroom, opening and closing drawers. I know what those discontented closet sounds mean.

"Max called," she says.

"Who's—" But I catch myself. "Band Guy. Right."

She makes a noise somewhere between a sigh and a grunt.

"So what's up?" I stand in front of the refrigerator and contemplate getting a snack. It takes me at least thirty seconds to notice the fridge has been replaced. It was stainless steel this morning; now it's all glass. You can see right through. Count how many apples are in the bin without even opening the thing.

"He invited me to some gig in Williamsburg."

"Mm-hmm." I'm staring at a bunch of grapes and the nectarines. My mother has belonged to a fruit-of-the-month club since before I was born. Once a month piles of pears or kiwis or pomegranates show up on our doorstep. She never eats them, and they usually just sit there until they turn and someone has to throw them away.

"Jesus, Caggs, do I have to beg? You're coming with me."

I open my mouth to protest, but I honestly can't think of a single excuse. I have too much homework? Not true: I have none. I have to spend time with Trevor? That go-to has definitely expired. I've been working on my honesty this summer. I've told such a big lie, such a massively irreversible one, that I figure I need to somehow even the score. But the thing about lying is that it's not so easy to stop. Lies need one another, like a school of fish. If you start to separate them, they'll be killed off one by one. Sometimes the only way to keep lies alive is to tell more of them.

"Okay," I say. "I'll come."

Claire screeches, victorious. It's obvious she thought she was going to have to gun way harder for me to come out tonight.

"I'll be down at like six." I say.

"Can you wear your red bandage dress?" she asks.

"Sure," I say. Claire gave me this Hervé Léger fire-engine-red, skin-tight dress for my birthday. I'm born on the Fourth of July, so her reasoning was incredibly specific: "Your attitude is blue, your skin is white, and this dress is red. It's perfect." But it's so tight it makes me feel like I'm being put through a juicer. There's no way I'm putting that thing on.

"Are we going to have fun tonight?" Her tone is pointed, and I can't help but smile. This is Claire's role. Throughout last year, through the spring, Claire was always the one who didn't take BS. Trevor, he was the one who held me when I cried, and asked me how I was doing, and tucked my chin against his chest, but not Claire. Claire's job has always been to remind me that life moves on. To keep heading forward. And she takes it pretty seriously.

"Damn straight," I say, which makes her laugh.

"Six!" she calls, and hangs up.

I take the grapes out. I was right—there are twenty-six.

I get to Claire's at six thirty. Usually she feels I am not wearing enough makeup or my clothes aren't "fun" enough and we have to go through the process of making both me and her happy (not the easiest of tasks). So it's best to show up late to avoid as much of this as possible.

"I didn't know we were swinging by church first. Excellent." Claire scans my outfit—dark jeans, white tank top and this Native American necklace my mom bought me on a

REBECCA SERLE

trip to Paris. My mom is always doing things like purchasing Native American necklaces in *Paris*.

I push past her. The inside of their apartment smells like garlic and wine. I can hear water being drained in the kitchen and the soft sounds of Etta James.

"Hey, Mrs. Howard," I call out.

"Darling!" Claire's mom comes around the corner, a dish towel in hand. She's a small woman with jet-black hair that she keeps in this longish bob. Today she looks like Audrey Hepburn: cigarette pants, white button-down, and neck scarf.

"How are you doing, sweetheart?" She pulls me into a hug, and I let myself get wrapped up in her smell—garlic and ginger and the faint hints of vanilla perfume.

"I'm good," I say. "You know, same old."

She eyes me. "Your mother?"

I shrug. "The usual."

She nods and flips the dish towel over her shoulder. She looks at Claire—Claire in her leather vest and cutoff denim shorts. "I'm taking it you're not staying for dinner?"

"We can't," Claire says, snatching my hand and dragging me toward the door. "We have to support Max."

I glance back apologetically at Mrs. Howard.

Max? she mouths to me.

I roll my eyes: *No big deal. Who knows. Claire.*

"Ten!" she calls after us.

The elevator delivers us downstairs and Claire puts up her hand to hail a cab. "No L train?" I ask, half kidding. Claire never takes the subway.

"Not in heels," she says.

A yellow cab slows and she ushers me inside. "Grand and Roebling," she says. "Williamsburg."

Claire starts prattling about how DJs are the new chefs, or something, and I lean back on the black plastic of the cab. I love the drive from Manhattan to Brooklyn, when the city is behind you, and you can appreciate it as this singular thing, this unit: Manhattan. It's pretty astounding. Even for someone like me, who's lived here her whole life. I know people joke that New York is the center of the world, but sometimes, on the bridge, it feels true. Like everything and anything of significance takes place right here in my hometown.

The entrance to the bar is hidden. It's sandwiched between a nail salon and a deli, and the door is plain wood, unmarked. Claire opens it and we walk down a hallway and then a small flight of stairs. It's not until we're on the stairs that I begin to hear the music—or maybe not so much hear as feel. The ground hums and vibrates below us like there's a locked dragon who is growing restless in his dungeon.

The bouncer eyes us and we flash our driver's licenses. They're fake, but we've had them for two years and they work pretty well. We rarely get turned away, which I think has more to do with Claire's connections—and legs—than the quality of our IDs. I bought them in Rhode Island when we went with Peter to look at Brown years ago. All I remember from that trip is that the three of us went to Start, this crazy dance party, and that we came home with these.

Whether it's Claire's legs or the IDs' appearance of validity I don't know, but they work again tonight. The bouncer nods us through.

When we get inside, it's dark and loud, but not loud enough that you have to scream to talk. It's still early. Max is onstage already, but Claire wants to get a drink. We slide our way to the bar. It's funny, I've had a fake ID since I was fifteen, but I've never used it for anything besides getting into places. Drinking really isn't my thing. I got drunk with Claire once, last summer at the beach house. Everyone was away and it was just the two of us. Trevor was supposed to come up, but he got stuck babysitting his little brother. My sister was in the city with my mom, Peter was on some postgrad safari, and my dad was probably away on business, I don't remember.

Anyway, we got bombed. We drank champagne straight from the bottle. We had like one each, I think. At a certain point it got a little fuzzy. I woke up on the sofa in the morning and my head felt like it had been hammered with an iron rod. I could barely even see.

"Why did we do that?" I remember asking Claire.

She just shrugged. "Because we did."

Claire doesn't spend too much time considering consequences, but this quality isn't incongruent with the rest of her. She's all angles—sharp elbows, cheekbones, and the point where adventure meets danger—like two walls of the same room. Nothing is cloudy with her. Nothing is round. Nothing needs too much time to decide. She's like a dart shot right through the bull's eye—if she's playing, it's all or nothing.

"Orange juice." Claire hands me a cup and takes a sip of hers—cranberry vodka, her usual drink.

She starts bobbing to the music. "They're pretty good, right?" she says to me.

I smile to say yes, but the truth is I don't know. I have no idea what makes good music. My iTunes collection is embarrassingly dated—some classics and Top 40 stuff. Whatever I end up stumbling into on Spotify and whatever Trevor introduced me to. The indie music scene is totally above my head. I just don't have the sensitivity for it. Or the ear. Most of it sounds the same to me. Claire and Trevor are always saying things like music is poetry—you're not supposed to dissect its meaning; you're just supposed to feel it—but that's my problem: I can't feel it. Or if I do, I'm never sure I'm having the right reaction.

"You're oblivious," Claire says to me.

I roll my eyes.

She repeats it, so close I can feel the words traveling down my ear canal, bouncing around on the walls.

I mock glare at her. "Just because I don't appreciate these hipsters the same way you do . . ."

She shakes her head and grabs my shoulders, turning me fifteen degrees to the left.

"What?" I ask.

She rolls her eyes and points to a guy at the end of the bar. He's leaning against the counter, like he's having a conversation with the bartender, but it's obvious he's looking at us. He raises his glass and eyebrows at the same time when we look over.

"Gross," I say. "He's old."

It's not true; he's probably no older than twenty. In fact, he might even be our age, but he's got that air. I know it. A lot of guys at Kensington have it. It's what happens when you spend your childhood being raised by a nanny, taking a car service by yourself at eight. It's what happens when your parents let you wander the city alone at ten, send you on a plane to visit your grandmother in the South of France or your father in Italy. You grow up faster. Not maturitywise, not at all, but something in the way you move. Those experiences age you. Seeing things, even bad things—especially bad things—that ages you.

Claire bites her lip and tosses her shoulders back. I grab her arm. "What are you doing?"

I've been the victim of Claire's flirtations before, and it's never something I wind up loving. One particular incident in Cabo comes to mind. We were on vacation with her parents in the spring of our sophomore year. After a night at our hotel, we ended up back at the villa of these two college guys. University of Wisconsin, classic frat boys. Popped collars, crew cuts, the whole bit. I hadn't wanted to go, but Claire had begged me, and as soon as we got there, she disappeared with one, the one she had been flirting with all night. I was stuck out on some lawn chairs with the other one. He was nice—I was lucky; he didn't even try to kiss me—but I was still so angry at Claire. I was with Trevor at the time, and I was so pissed at her for putting me in that position that I didn't talk to her the entire rest of the trip. It was only when we were headed home, on the plane, that she turned to me, these pink sparkly sunglasses on. They were bedazzled, and across the top were the words "I LOVE CAGGIE." It was an impressive feat, for being in Mexico, and I couldn't help myself—I popped them off her face and onto mine.

"We're here for Band Guy, remember?" I say to her.

"This isn't for me; it's for you," she says, still smiling at the bar guy.

"I doubt he's going to come over for me," I say. "You're practically giving him a lap dance from across the room."

Claire's head snaps around to look at me. "I've had it," she says.

"What?"

"This." She contorts her face, sticking her bottom lip out and making her eyes big like puppies'.

"I don't know what you're referring to."

She slings her arm over my shoulder. "Come on, Caggs, it's time to move on. Trevor was great, and totally adorable in that clueless kind of way"—she tilts her head to the side, like she's pulling up his image in her mind's eye—"but he's old news. Kaput. *Finito.* E*xtravaganza.* You dig me?"

"I dig you."

"So flirt a little," she says, giving me a push toward Bar Man. "What's the worst that could happen?"

Great question.

So I step forward. It only takes one for Mr. Bar Man to come toward me. As he gets closer, I see that I'm right: He's about my age, maybe a little bit older. He's dressed well—tailored shirt, black pants—and he's got dark, dark hair and eyes. Even inside, in this poorly lit music hall, it's easy to spot that they're so brown they're almost black.

"Well," he says when we're within speaking distance. "This is a surprise. Nice to see you."

I frown. "Excuse me?"

He doesn't answer, just keeps looking at me. It makes the back of my neck feel hot.

"Do we know each other?" I ask.

I cross my arms. He runs his tongue over his top lip. "We used to."

I feel my heartbeat quicken. I hadn't actually expected him to say yes. I thought he meant that he was surprised I came over. Or that I wasn't Claire.

"You look perturbed," he says.

I shake my head. "I don't think we do."

He takes a sip of his drink. Sets it down. Exhales. "We do."

"Well, I have no idea who you are. No offense or anything."

He smiles. "I wouldn't expect you to. It was a long time ago. You're Mcalister, right?"

More heart pounding. "Yes."

"Of the Caulfields?"

Ah. Yes. "Do you know me, or have you just heard of me?"

He whistles. "Impressive. Spunky. I like that. No, I went to school with your brother. Patrick?"

"Peter."

"Right. Nice kid."

"You didn't go to Kensington," I say. My brother was only two grades ahead of me, and I knew everyone in his class, more or less.

"Grammar school," he says. "We've been in London for the last few years."

"Oh." That makes sense. My brother went to Prep until the ninth grade, so we were in different schools. Prep is all boys, and a lot of them choose to go to middle school there instead of Wheatley. Prep doesn't go all the way through, though, so they all transfer in.

My shoulders start to drop a little. "You recognized me?"

He tilts his head to the side. "I have a pretty good memory." I feel his eyes loop my face. "You always used to come with your mom to pick your brother up. You haven't changed very much."

I shake my head. "You have no idea."

"You want a drink?" he asks.

I motion to the orange juice in my hand.

"There's no alcohol in there," he says.

"No?" I bring the cup to my lips.

"No way," he says. "You're not a vodka girl." He motions for the bartender. "Two whisky sours," he says. To me: "You'll like it. I promise."

"What do you promise?" I ask. I'm feeling just a little bit flirtatious. Maybe it's all the vitamin C. More likely the fact that I can practically feel Claire's eyes boring into me and her voice: *Can't you ever just* pretend *to have fun?*

"I don't make contingency plans," he says. "Just trust me."

He takes out a lighter and flicks the flame up. It startles me and I blink, taking a step backward.

"You can't smoke in here," I say. Stupid. Childish. Like a little kid tattling. So much for the witty.

He snaps the lighter closed. "I don't smoke."

"What's your name, anyway?" I ask, changing the subject.

"Astor."

"Astor what?"

He cocks his head to the side. "Did I stumble into a game of twenty questions?"

I suddenly feel silly. I don't even know why I'm talking to him. Because Claire pushed me over? "So London, huh?" I say, taking a gulp of OJ. "Did you just move back?"

"Few months ago."

"You're in college?" I ask.

He looks at me, takes a swig of one of the drinks that have just been set down. "Not right now."

"Right. Because right now you're here at this bar. I get it." I shake my head.

He laughs. "That's not what I mean. I'm not going right now."

"Okay," I say, bringing my glass up to my lips.

He peers at me. "Surprised?"

I shrug. "Not really. A little unusual, I guess, for someone like you."

A smile cracks along his face. Like a knife carving a pumpkin. "Someone like me?"

"Come on," I say. "You know what I mean."

He nods. "I do indeed." He sets his drink down. "So you think I'm wild?"

"No," I say.

"Adventurous?" he tries. He angles his body so it's facing me, and flicks the straw out of my drink onto the counter. For some reason it makes me self-conscious. I run my pinky down the side of my glass, scooping up a bead of condensation.

"I don't know," I say. "I don't know you. But I get it, I think."

"Not many people do."

I look up at him. "I'm not most people."

He holds my gaze for a moment, and something passes between us. Something you can't see, just feel. Then he laughs and the mood lightens. "Noted."

"So," I say. "What *are* you doing now?"

"Like tonight?" He winks at me and runs a hand through his hair. I can't help but notice his fingers—long and lean, like him. He has a leather bracelet on his wrist, with a tiny silver clasp. "I get that college is what I'm supposed to be doing, but it's not for me. Not now, anyway. I kind of have a different way of looking at the future."

"Oh yeah?"

He smiles. "Yeah. Here." He hands me my drink. I take it. "So what's your take?" I ask.

He turns and leans against the bar. "It's just never seemed as certain to me as it has to other people." He takes another sip. Stops. "Like these boxes people keep ticking. High school. College. Work. Marriage. Kids. How can you be so sure you'll make it to the next one?"

"I know what you mean."

He eyes me, like he's trying to determine whether that's true or not. "Yeah?"

"Trust me," I say. "Yes."

"Okay, then, Mcalister Caulfield. Let's toast." He raises his glass, and I surprise myself by doing the same. Then he looks me square in the eye. There's a lot in that look. It's enticing, nerve-racking. Like a roller coaster that you know is going to make your heart plummet down into your stomach, but it must be what you want, because you get on anyway. "To now," he says.

We clink; ice cubes rattle. Then I take a sip. The alcohol burns a trail down my throat. It feels good. Hot. Like a brushfire. Like it's clearing something out.

CHAPTER FIVE

"Why do you hate me so much?" my mother asks. We're at Bergdorf's, browsing around the hat department. It's on the ground floor, close to the doors. I like to stay near exits when I'm shopping with my mom. I'm also very inconsistently listening to Claire's lunch date. Her dad made her go out with some aspiring photographer, one of his assistants, and she made me promise to come along—cellularly.

"I don't hate *you*," I say. "I hate that hat."

My mom gives me a look that seems to say, *Same difference.* She has a tendency to overidentify.

This is usually what shopping is like with her. She wants me to dress like Abigail or Constance or one of the other girls in my grade who take off ten thousand dollars' worth of accessories and store them in their lockers when we have gym. It's ridiculous. There are children starving in Africa, and my mother is concerned about a Chloé dress. You'd think that after my sister died, she would have gotten some perspective, that this stuff would have become far less important to her, but that's not at all what happened. It was the opposite. She redecorated our house after eighteen months, same as always. She bought a whole new wardrobe. Sometimes I think she feels like the real world abandoned her, so she might as well stay here: in cotton and Lycra and linen.

"I like this," I offer. I pull up a summer scarf. It's cream colored with big stitching.

My mother ignores the gesture. "I spoke to your brother," she says.

"Peter?"

"Any other siblings I should know about?"

We both get a little quiet. She clears her throat. "He said he's thinking of coming home next weekend."

I set the scarf back and in the process knock a bag off a mannequin. I reach down and fumble with picking it back up. "Already? He just got there."

"Felicia," my mother says.

"Right."

"I don't think she's any good for him," she says, sashaying over to the jewelry case.

I trot behind. "No? I dunno. He loves her and all."

My mother looks at me sharply, like I've just sworn. "She's a distraction," she says.

"From what? Other girls?"

I put the phone up to my ear and hear Claire laugh. It's genuine, so I know things are going fine. Plus I don't think this is getting romantic. She's still with Max, and it's lunch.

"Don't be smart," my mother says. She motions for the saleslady to let her see a ring. It's blue. Sapphire. She barely even looks at it before she nods to wrap it up.

"So look, Mom, I'm probably late to meet Claire." That's a lie—Claire is obviously busy at the moment—but we're getting increasingly farther away from the exit, which means I'm starting to sweat in here. And that's a feat. It's always freezing in Bergdorf's.

"We're having lunch," she says. "Claire can come if she'd like." She taps her finger on the glass counter.

I pick up the phone again. "Demarchelier is my godfather, actually," I hear Claire say.

"You know Trevor came by again yesterday," my mother says.

Instantly my heart starts racing. I glance downward, toward the jewelry case. "Why?" I ask.

"What do you mean, why?"

"He must have had a reason. Why else would he come

over?" I can feel my neck start to heat up. I keep my face pointed low.

"He told me you wouldn't speak to him," she says, fingering a gold bracelet. "He said he didn't have a choice."

"He came to talk to you?" For just a moment, my confusion eclipses my anxiety. This conversation is unusual for a few reasons. Lately my mom isn't too aware of what's going on in our house. Frankly, I wasn't even sure she knew Trevor and I had broken up. Also, my mom and I have never had that mother-daughter relationship where we tell each other everything. It isn't our thing. She's always just sort of let me live. I didn't come to her when I was thinking of sleeping with Trevor. We don't lie in bed together and talk about love. We're not like that. If we ever were, we certainly aren't now.

"No," she said. "He was hoping to catch you."

"He's becoming a master of the ambush," I say under my breath.

"You two were close," my mother says, like she hasn't heard me.

"Yeah, we were." I busy myself with a counter display of dangly earrings.

"Are you seeing anyone else?" she asks.

The question startles me, and so does Astor's face flashing across my mind without warning. To Claire's disappointment I didn't give him my number. In my defense, he didn't ask. I had a feeling if I offered it he would have said something like *If it's meant to be, we'll see each other again.* But we haven't. Not in the last four days, anyway. It's just that he keeps showing up in my head unannounced.

"No," I say. "It's not like Kensington is crawling with great guys." That's true, too. Who am I going to date? Tripp? Even he is taken.

My mother raises her eyebrows. "I think there are a lot of fine young men at Kensington. Some of the best—"

I hold up my hand. "Mom, I'd rather wear gingham for the rest of my life than date someone named Archibald. Or Walter. Or Harrington." I swear, every guy I know has a name that makes him sound like he could be my grandfather. Well, not *my* grandfather, but *a* grandfather. You get what I mean. And I guess, really, Astor is no exception. Except something about him felt like an exception. Something about him felt different.

"What's wrong with gingham?" For a moment I think she's made a joke, but I'm wrong. She legitimately wants to know.

"Let's just go to lunch," I say.

"You've never been to LA?" Claire screeches when I pick up my cell to check in. They're probably not getting married anytime soon, but it doesn't seem like she's in any

THE EDGE OF FALLING

immediate danger. I decide to hang up and face lunch head-on.

There is this restaurant, Phoebe's, on East Sixty-Seventh, that my mom has been going to for years. Phoebe's never ceases to depress me. For one, the food is terrible and yet the place is always packed. Sometimes the line for a table spills out to the sidewalk. For another, no one eats there. Not really. They have this caprese salad that tastes like rubber, and their sandwiches are sand infused. I'm not sure why it's so popular, but it is, so people go. That's the thing about the neighborhood I live in: Rarely does anyone stop to question why they're doing the things they're doing. It's a good enough reason if everyone else is.

When we get to Phoebe's, Abigail is seated at a table with Constance and Samantha. Unsurprising. They are always here on Sundays.

"Mcalister!" Abigail calls out when she sees me.

My mother slides her sunglasses up on top of her head and gives me an eye. Abigail is never this friendly to me in public. Even my mother knows that.

"Hey." I wave at them, searching desperately for a table on the other side of the restaurant. Too late. Abigail calls us over with her hand, and my mother, God help her, goes. I drag my feet behind.

R
E
B
E
C
C
A

S
E
R
L
E

Abigail air-kisses my mom and then turns to me. "What *are* you doing here?"

"Lunch?" I say. "The meal before dinner?"

Abigail misses the sarcasm, but not my mother. She tucks her arm around my waist and pulls.

"Are you girls doing International this year?" my mother asks. She's talking about the debutante ball that's held at the Waldorf Astoria every other year. She's been trying to get me to agree to it since before I can remember. I don't see the point in putting on a big white dress and strutting around with people I can't stand, but my mother thinks it's more important than a wedding. We're in negotiations.

"My mom wants me to do Junior Assemblies," Abigail says. "Which means I might wait until next year—but I'm *so* ready!"

"Mayflower," Constance says. "Vera is already fitting me."

"Maybe you can help me convince this one?" My mother looks pointedly at me and then at Constance.

Abigail sighs. I notice she's wearing an orange dress that clashes wildly with her red curls. She looks like a surrealist painting, the kind you sometimes have to step away from to see what the hell is going on. "Honestly, Caggie, it's unheard of not to come out."

"By who?" I ask. My mother's hand pinches my waist.

Constance rolls her eyes. "Everyone?"

"I'll work on it," Abigail tells my mother, like even the thought is exhausting. "Speaking of, we were just discussing some school politics."

"Super," I say. "We really should—"

"The new boy," Constance says, piping up. She has a cardigan draped over her shoulders like she's afraid of catching cold. It's 101 degrees outside.

"What new boy?" This from my mother. I swear her ears perk right up with her eyebrows.

"A transfer," Samantha says. "We hear he's from Dubai."

Abigail snorts. "He is not from *Dubai*," she corrects. "He's been living in Venice."

"He went to jail," Constance says.

"He speaks five languages," Abigail adds.

"That's quite a lot of things," my mother says.

Abigail adjusts her headband like she's looking in a mirror, but instead she's looking straight at me. "I think I might make him my boyfriend."

"Oh?" I say. "I thought things were good with Tripp."

Abigail inhales. "He just isn't coming around the way I want him to."

She lowers her eyes to her hands. My mother reaches out and gives them a sympathetic squeeze.

"Right," I say. "So listen, we really should—"

"I think Caggie could use a distraction," my mother

announces. She's still holding me by the waist, and she tugs me closer again.

Abigail's eyes light up. "Oh, *yes*," she says.

"It's been a long summer, right, sweetie?" my mother continues.

I close my eyes, briefly. I resist the urge to run screaming from this restaurant. "Two and a half months," I say. "Pretty standard."

My mother ignores this. "Maybe you girls could see if the new boy has any friends." She winks at Abigail. I want to crawl under the table and just evaporate.

"Done," Abigail says. "Maybe I'll have a back-to-school party," she continues. "We could invite him." She looks at Constance, who takes out a notebook.

The thought of any party of Abigail's makes my bones feel like they've turned to lead. Kristen—her tiny, breakable frame—replaces Astor's image.

My mother releases me, claps her hands together. "I've always adored you, Abbey."

I snort. It's almost enough to make me forget the possibility of another Abigail Adams soiree. She doesn't let her hatred of her nickname show now, though. Instead she just stands and air-kisses my mother again, once on each cheek.

"All right, darlings," my mom says, passing a hand over the table in an arched wave. "We'll leave you be."

"I'll call you," Abigail says, although it's unclear whether she's referring to me or my mother.

"See you tomorrow," I say.

As we leave, I hear them drop their voices, probably discussing my wardrobe choice or the size of my mother's diamond ring. I've never known girls like that to be too kind in private.

"That was fun!" my mother says. I can tell she really means it, and I don't say anything to correct her. The truth is my mom doesn't find much fun these days, not since Hayley. So if Abigail really revs her up, who am I to shut that down?

"I always liked that girl," she continues. "I think you guys should be friends."

"We are," I say. At least Abigail thinks so.

Over lunch we talk about Peter (he should break up with Felicia), Claire (I should stop "running downtown" to see her; it takes me out of my life), and Dad (she's not sure when he's coming home from his trip; I feel like adding "if," but don't).

Abigail & Co. blow us even more air kisses as they leave. They glide by in their stilettos and wedges, bags clutched in their hands, sunglasses fixed on their faces. I wonder if their internal dialogue would surprise me. If they ever think things they don't say. I kind of doubt it.

I take a sip of my lemonade and watch as the ice cubes

play bumper cars in the glass. "Peter said you're selling the house," I venture. I don't know why I choose now to bring it up. I don't blame my mother for not telling me, not exactly, but I still want to talk about it. I know it wasn't a group decision. It's not my house; it's my parents'. But I still feel like it's not right to sell it off. She's still there, in a way, isn't she?

My mother sets her chardonnay down. "Yes," she says, folding her hands on the table. "Why?"

I give my lemonade a shake. "I just figured someone might have mentioned something, that's all."

"Your brother was kind enough to volunteer to pack up," my mother says, her tone crisp. "There isn't really anything to say, Mcalister."

"I would have gone," I say. I'm surprised that I say it. I was mad at Peter for being out there all summer; I considered it a betrayal.

My mother looks at me and I see something hard in her eyes. Something that is, now, familiar. "That wouldn't have been a good idea," she says.

I know what she means. I know what she's referring to. But it still makes me feel cold. Like I've swallowed all the ice cubes in my glass in one swoop. The last time I was at the beach was the night Hayley died.

I was the only one with her that night. We weren't supposed to be out there, but I had planned a weekend with

Trevor, and if all went according to plan, no one would find out. My parents had some benefit and Peter was in the city, spending the weekend with Felicia. Hayley was supposed to be home with the nanny, but the nanny had gotten sick at the last minute and couldn't make it into the city. Hayley begged to come with me. She loved the beach, even in winter. Especially in winter. She would sit outside, all bundled up in scarves and sweaters and coats, and she would paint, her little hand shaking from the cold, from being the only piece of skin on her body exposed besides her nose.

I said yes. To her coming with, I mean. Trevor was going to take the train out Saturday and maybe Claire, too, if she could pull herself away from whomever she was dating at the time. One of her dad's assistants, I think. An up-and-coming rock-and-roll photographer with a name like Craw or Sebastian—I can't remember.

Hayley and I drove out together Friday night. We listened to Bob Marley in the car. Hayley said it made her feel like it was summer even though the roads were icy and frost kept forming on the windshield. She played with this bracelet the whole way up. It was an evil-eye bracelet Trevor had given me for our one-year anniversary. Blue glass beads all around. "It's protection," he told me. "So you'll always be safe." I had let her have it. Not permanently or anything—it didn't even fit her yet—but I let her wear it that night. She kept spinning it around, running her little fingers over the tiny black dots in the centers of the blue beads.

I remember we talked about her field trip. She was upset that her class was going to the New Museum downtown. She thought it shouldn't count as a field trip if you stayed in Manhattan. She wanted to know whether I'd help her make a petition. She wanted to inform the school and see how many people she could get to sign. That's the kind of kid Hayley was. She was always speaking her mind, letting people know how she felt. She'd say anything. She'd tell people she loved them every time they left the room.

We got to the house and she started carrying in her suitcase. It was just a little duffel with her initials stenciled on it, but it was hard for her. Hayley was tiny. Barely four foot two, and bone thin. I remember her struggling with it a little, but I didn't help her. I had my hands full, and besides, I reasoned, Hayley wasn't complaining. She would have gotten mad at me too, if I had taken it out of her hands. She was like that. She thought she could do anything.

But she couldn't swim. She hadn't learned how.

Hayley was afraid of the water; I'm not really sure why. When she was a baby she would scream whenever anyone tried to bathe her. She took showers and everything, that's not what I mean, but she never wanted to go in the ocean.

Even when she was little, she would stay way up on the sand dunes. She would build castles and lie around with her shovel and bucket, but she never wandered down to the edge.

I used to try to get her to tell me, but she didn't want to talk about it. She was like an adult who had had a scarring experience and didn't want to rehash the past. I sometimes thought it was funny. She was just ten, after all; what had traumatized her so much? But that's the thing about kids that's so interesting. It's true about Peter and me and it's true about any child who has ever been born to parents. Hayley was who she was. It didn't much have anything to do with what had happened to her in her short life. Maybe people can be afraid of the future. Maybe she saw what was coming.

I blink and look at my mom. She looks tired, older. I can see the lines around her eyes stretching like highways on a flat-pressed map. Roads well traveled.

"I'm going to go have a rest," she says. "Will you stay out or come home?"

I glance down at my watch: two forty-five. If this was last year, I'd be crossing the park. I'd meet Trevor on Sixty-Sixth and we'd pick up Starbucks and go for a walk, or if it was really hot, too hot, we'd go back to his apartment, close all the blinds, and turn the AC on full blast.

"I have some homework," I lie. "I'll come back with you."

We walk in silence. Sometimes this happens without warning. Like the magnitude of the past—of all that has happened—creeps into the space and inflates. One minute it's this little thing—contained, pocket-size—the next minute it's a creature. With legs and arms and scales. That's how grief works. It's there even when you forget about it. It doesn't disappear, but just morphs, changes form.

Hayley might have screamed, but I didn't hear her, so I don't know. She probably did, but our house is on the water, and it's windy outside at night most of the time. Sound gets swallowed.

It was fifteen minutes before I found her. I was opening the door to call her inside. Fifteen minutes was too long to spend outside in January. It was freezing. But Hayley liked to look at the moon. She'd say things like "I'm getting inspired," so I hadn't immediately stopped her when she had opened the sliding glass doors. It would have been a fight. She was sweet, but she was also stubborn.

I called her but she didn't answer. Then I stuck my head out. I had taken my coat off, and the wind hit me—sharp as knives. Something dropped in my stomach then, like a coin in a slot machine. I swear I heard it rattle. This wasn't right. It was too biting cold for her to have stayed out this long. I started calling her name madly, like those frantic mothers you see in malls who have lost their toddlers. "Hayley!" "Hayley!" I screamed it.

I turned on all the lights. I ran around the back and stared down at the ocean. I turned around and tried to see into the dark house, the living room, the kitchen, down to where our bedrooms are. Nothing.

And then I saw it. My bracelet. The evil eyes winking at me from the bottom of the swimming pool, five tiny fingers trailing next to it, a fist unclenched.

There was a lot of explanation later. About cold-water drowning and the brain dying and hypothermia and the difference between six minutes and ten. It had been fifteen. Fifteen full minutes that I did nothing. Fifteen full minutes that I loaded boxes of macaroni and cheese into the kitchen cabinet and turned on the television. They told me there was nothing I could have done, those were their words, but the research said something else. Their medical voices said something else. I could have. I could have realized my little sister was gone. I could have caught her when she fell in, trying to fish out my bracelet. My stupid, meaningless bracelet. I could have pulled back the pool covering so she wouldn't have been caught in it. I could have rescued her in the first thirty seconds. The first minute. The first six. I could have stopped her from dying.

You see, now, why I do not want to talk about May. Why

I'm telling you out of sheer necessity. To cover the truth, I have to lie, but it's the guilt that is the worst. It's heavy, thick. It doesn't let me breathe. How can I claim responsibility for saving anyone when I let my sister die?

CHAPTER SIX

I recognize him immediately. His pink oxford and blazer with the Kensington crest stenciled on the front. The way his hair parts to the side, styled down that way. "You've got to be kidding me," I mutter. *He's* the new guy?

Astor is standing at the gates to school, one foot on the sidewalk of Fifth, another on campus, like he isn't committed to either world just yet. He's weighing his options. My pulse jumps a little when I see him, I'll admit it. I keep imagining him, envisioning his face at the bar, the memory of his glass clinking mine. It's embarrassing that I keep calling up his image. Especially because now he's really here.

I secure my book bag on my shoulder and walk over to him. Better to just nip this in the bud. Deal with it head-on.

"Look who it is," I say. I try to play it casual, cool, but something about him rattles me. Even my voice shakes a little.

He turns around. He's flicking his lighter off and on. His eyes travel from the flame up to my face. "You following me, Caulfield?"

I shake my head. "Nice try, but this is my turf."

"Mine too."

He smiles at me, and it all begins to make sense, like the last chapter of a book where the mystery is explained. "You didn't choose not to go to college; you got kicked out of high school," I say.

"So quick to jump to conclusions," Astor says, clucking his tongue and dropping the lighter into his pocket. "Maybe I simply want to further my education."

"*Have* to further your education," I correct. "My guess is you got busted for something, your London school said *sayonara*, Daddy wrote a big fat check to Kensington, and they agreed to take your tail for a repeat of senior year." I put my hands on my hips, triumphant.

He cocks his head to the side and looks at me. "Does it get hard?" he asks.

"What?"

"Thinking so much. You should rest that pretty head of yours occasionally, Caggs."

"How do you know my nickname?" I ask.

He shrugs. "You're a popular girl." He steps his second foot off Fifth onto the Kensington campus. "So what does one do around here for fun, anyway?"

"School?"

He rolls his eyes. "You think school is fun? I thought we were alike. Don't tell me I pegged you all wrong."

I cross my arms. "I doubt we're alike."

He raises his eyebrows. "You've got some secrets too. My guess is you don't love it here, it's not your jam."

I shift my bag on my shoulder. "And what would make you say that?"

He runs his eyes over my face and steps closer. I can smell him. Expensive cologne. Cinnamon. Thick and heady. "Because you're here right now, talking to me."

My head starts throbbing, the blood pumping strong in my temples.

He leans forward even more. So close now it should be illegal. On school grounds, at least. "Have dinner with me," he says.

"What?" I yank myself back. I blink a few times. It feels like I just went unconscious for a moment. Did he just ask me out?

He smiles. "Come on, it'll be fun."

"Dinner?"

"You've heard of the meal, no?"

I narrow my eyes at him. "Why?"

"Why not?" he asks.

"Why would you want to have dinner with me?"

He shrugs. "You seem tolerable. Slightly." He looks me up and down. "Plus I don't really know anyone at Kensington. I thought you could show me the ropes."

"Trust me, I don't know them." My heart is racing. I try to quiet it, but it's no good.

"I'll bet that's not all true." He leans forward again. "And I think we'd have fun together."

"I don't think so," I say, but something inside me has unlocked, loosened up. Maybe it's the cologne. God help me, I kind of want to say yes.

Then he turns away from me and strolls out of the Kensington gates. "I'll pick you up at six," he calls over his shoulder.

"Don't you have class?" I ask.

"It's history," he says. "We conquered some people. Some people died. Some art was made. I get the general picture. See you at six, sweetheart."

"Don't you need to know where I live?"

He spins and faces me, winks. "I'll be there," he says. "Have a little faith, Caggs."

My head is still foggy from Astor when I see Trevor in English. He manages to secure the desk next to me, and I can't pay attention. I feel distracted by everything. The pencil sharpener by the chalkboard, the stack of books on Mr. Tenner's desk. The clock, beating its way toward six.

I keep catching Trevor looking at me, and he's distracting too. The blue of his shirt, the curve of his arm. The way his fingers hold his pencil, his thumb wrapped around. I think about those hands. The beds of his fingers are dark, stained brown from working at George's Coffee House on Eighty-First and Amsterdam.

"Hey," he says.

I nod, but only meet his gaze for a moment. I look back down at my notebook.

When Kristen comes in, no one really makes a fuss about it. A few people look up, but they go back to checking out Blake Keeley's paparazzi photos—she's been snapped all over the park making out with that guy from the Disney Channel show about witches.

Kristen waves at me, and I wave back. So far so good. Maybe I can trust her after all.

I make it through the period, just barely, and manage to escape before Trevor can follow me.

At lunch I check my phone: one new message from Claire. *There are no chestnuts dwntwn.*

It makes me smile. Ever since I was little, I've always loved chestnuts. They sell them on the street uptown and they're delicious—roasted and unshelled. When the weather gets cold, I buy a bag a day. The best vendor is by the Plaza on Fifty-Ninth Street, but come fall you can pretty much find chestnuts anywhere uptown. When Claire first moved to Tribeca it was August, but unseasonably cold, and we were helping her unpack when I really wanted chestnuts. We went downstairs and wandered around a few blocks, but we couldn't find any. At the time, I was sad Claire had left the Upper East Side and I remember saying to her, all bitter and everything, "You see? There are no chestnuts downtown." She thought it was hilarious, and since then she'll say it for just about everything—when one of us can't find a restaurant or store we're searching for, and, she says, when she misses me. It's our code.

I wonder if they r in bklyn? I text back. She was supposed to see Max last night, but I haven't spoken to her yet. Needless to say, she didn't let me listen in.

My phone immediately lights up. *Need to give u details! Come over tnite??*

I jump to respond, but then pause. I shouldn't really consider this thing with Astor tonight. He's not even going to show up. He was kidding, I'm sure. But instead of telling Claire yes, what I actually write is: *fam stuff. Tmrw?*

Lame!

I drop my phone in the side pocket of my bag and check my watch. I can't believe the day is only halfway done.

"Hey, Caggie!" Abigail swings into the gates with Constance and Samantha behind. Her red curls bob next to her head like pulled Slinkys. "We missed you at lunch today."

"Sorry," I say. "Homework." For a preparatory academy that prides itself on being an Ivy League feeder school, I sure lie pretty often about the amount of work I have to do.

Abigail looks me up and down. "I saw you talking to Astor," she says to my stomach.

What is up with everyone seeing everyone else having conversations around here?

"Uh, yeah. He's . . . a friend."

That isn't even *slightly* true, but the words tumble out. Abigail makes her eyes wide.

"I thought he was new here," she says. She's fighting a smile, I can tell. She practically sings out the words.

"He is," I continue. "He's an old family friend." That's not technically, in fact, *un*true, seeing as how he told me he went to school with Peter. He also told me he was a high school graduate who had opted out of college, not someone who got kicked out of a London school. I suddenly feel kind of sick about bailing on Claire tonight.

Abigail gives a nod. "His family is loaded. Like European shipping money or something," she says.

"His dad was on the cover of *Forbes*," Constance adds.

"Since when do you read *Forbes*?" Samantha asks.

Abigail clears her throat and Constance rolls her eyes.

Abigail moves closer to me. "He's cute, don't you think?"

"Not really my type."

"It seemed like you're his."

I cross my arms. "Is there something you want to ask me, Abbey?"

Abigail narrows her eyes for a moment, and then her face breaks out into a smile, like some invisible string has pulled all her features outward. "Not at all! I just thought, with you and Trevor broken up, we might see you have some fun."

Constance and Samantha squeal beside her.

"Well, thanks, but I'm all good on the fun front." The chimes sound. "Gotta go. See you—" I dash off toward the math wing.

Abigail wants me to have fun. *Right.* This is clearly all part of some complicated ploy to keep Astor for herself—isn't that what Abigail said she wanted? He can be another prince to play house with.

For the record, she dated a real prince last year, in between Tripp. He was the heir of some tiny eastern European country that sounded like the name of a vampire, but he had a title. I'm not sure why they broke up, exactly, but it didn't last long. I know she didn't make it up, though. One thing about Abigail: It's easy to tell when she's lying.

*   *   *

By five thirty I'm home and checking my watch. I've changed out of my school uniform into jeans and a white top—I'd do that anyway, I remind myself—and washed my face. I've never been a big makeup person, to my mother's dismay, but I fish some lip gloss out of my bag and swipe it across a few times. It's just because they're chapped, I reason. The summer sun kills them.

At exactly six our doorbell rings. I've been hanging out in the foyer, flipping through a magazine in a chair. I'm not sure whether or not I knew he'd come, but I've been sitting here, haven't I? I didn't go visit Claire. Either way, the doorbell makes me jump. Now that he's actually on the other side, I'm not sure if I want to open it.

But I do, and as soon as I see Astor, my stomach jumps, like a frog on a lily pad. He's on the second step, wearing jeans and a white button-down, his hair gelled up a bit at the top. It's obvious he spent some time on this look, and I don't feel guilty anymore about my run-in with the lip gloss.

He smiles. "You're here."

"I live here."

He slips a hand behind his neck and pulls. It does something funny to the back of my neck too. "I'm happy you answered."

I bite my lip. Keep it cool, Mcalister.

"I just thought you might leave me hanging," he continues.

I inhale. Instinctively, I think about making up an excuse. It's like second nature lately, or something. "Yeah, well, I'm about to. I have all this homework . . . ," I start.

He shakes his head. "No way. School just started. You can't con a pro, Caggs."

I sigh. "Just come in, okay?"

"I thought you'd never ask."

I hold the door open, and he walks in past me. He brushes up against me, and when he does, my pulse seems to lurch forward, like an airplane taking off. "Nice place," he says.

"How did you find it, anyway?" I ask.

"I remembered." He looks at me until I look away. "I've never been inside."

I blow some air out my lips. "Do you want a drink or something?" I ask.

"Scotch?" He peers around the door that leads to the kitchen.

"I meant water."

He looks back at me. Laughs. "I was kidding."

"I know." I run my toe through the carpet. It's got this geometric print on it, and I try to follow in a semicircle using my pinky toe. Another thing my mom changed about our house this year.

"Are you hungry?" he asks me.

I glance up. He's staring at me. His eyes are gorgeous. He'd be hard to miss, he really would. "Sure."

"Italian?"

"Whatever."

He laughs. "I like a girl with a strong opinion." He strains again toward the kitchen. "Do you have to tell anyone you're leaving?"

I shake my head. "Nah. My mom won't be home until later." I don't mention Dad . . . no point. He isn't here, and if he was . . . well, I don't think my safety is of the utmost concern to him right now.

"Okay. Let's go." He takes one final sweep of the foyer, like he's surveying it. Then he nods, pulling the door open. He holds it for me and then tugs it shut behind him. It locks automatically.

It's still light outside. Still summer. "Do you want to walk?" he asks me.

"Okay," I say.

He holds out his elbow. I loop my arm through.

My arm feels funny in his. Small, maybe. He's tall, taller than Trevor. Most people are taller than me, but there seems to be something particularly towering about him as we head down Madison.

It suddenly occurs to me that I may be on a date with

Astor and I actually don't know a thing about him.

"Where do you live?" I ask.

"Sixty-Eighth and Lex." He holds up his hand to keep a taxi at bay as we cross the street.

"How come you moved to London?" I try.

"My dad has business," he says, without missing a beat.

"How come you got kicked out of school?"

Astor blows some air out of his lips. "They were teaching crap there, so I took matters into my own hands."

"Sounds ominous."

"It's not," he says, looking at me. "It wasn't my first high school, anyway."

"No?"

"Look," he says, "what's important is that I'm here now. No London, no getting kicked out, no meeting you."

I feel myself blush, but I still say: "Isn't that what you do on a date? Get to know someone?" I bite my tongue as soon as the words are out. Is this a date? Did I just seriously say that out loud?

He looks amused, though. "I don't really like talking about myself. I'd rather hear about you."

"I pretty much feel the same way, actually."

"Yeah? But you're so interesting." He hangs on the last word and unhooks his arm through mine. He rests his hand on the small of my back. I let him.

"I'm not," I say. "Trust me."

"I guess we'll agree to disagree." He puts up his hand to hail a passing cab, and the next thing I know, his fingers are at my waist and he's tucking me inside.

"Hudson and Perry," he tells the driver.

Astor positions himself close to me, and as we head downtown, he doesn't slide over. His breath seems even, calm, but mine comes short and shallow. I'm sure he can feel my heartbeat—quick and erratic. He moves his leg away from mine, takes his lighter out of his pocket.

"What's with that?" I ask.

"What?"

I motion with my head to the lighter in his hands. "You don't even smoke."

"So what?" he says.

"So why do you always have it?"

The flame ignites and he holds it out to me. Like he's offering it. "Don't you ever like to play with fire?"

It makes my pulse race again. The combination of his arrogance and—what? Charm?—is strangely alluring. He doesn't know enough about me for me to have to lie. Or be honest. And lately, anyway, they've seemed like the same thing.

We eat at a bistro where Astor knows everyone. I'm used to this; it happens every time Claire and I go out. Bottles of champagne get sent to our table, free chocolate soufflés show up with raspberry syrup wound into words around the sides of the plates. Sometimes numbers. Phone numbers. Claire always rolls her eyes like it's an inconvenience, but secretly I know she loves it. I feel another pang of guilt about not seeing her tonight, but I brush it to the side. Not now.

The food here is delicious. Pasta with shrimp and pesto. Big plates of handmade mozzarella and fresh tomatoes.

"What really happened?" I ask, twirling some spaghetti around a fork. "With school, I mean. How come you got kicked out? At Kensington you have to basically commit murder for them to even consider making someone leave. It taints their perfect record."

He folds his napkin onto the table and leans back in his chair. "I guess London rolls different. It wasn't anything glamorous; I just didn't show up." He holds up his hands. "Okay, also, I may have called a teacher something I shouldn't have."

I imagine Astor having it out with Principal Calleher. It makes me snort with laugher.

"Oh, good," he says. "You think it's funny. Most people just think I'm a delinquent."

"You're not a delinquent," I say automatically.

He raises his eyebrows. The flame from a candle on the table dances across his face.

"I just mean," I continue, "I'm not one to judge."

He runs his eyes over my face, like he's trying to read something there. Then he drops his gaze to his water glass. "Anyway, as long as I don't miss seven classes or get below a C here, I'll graduate."

"Seems easy enough."

"Especially if you're there." He takes my hand. He just reaches across the table and loops his fingers through mine.

I've never been out with anyone but Trevor. Well, there was Harrington freshman year, but that hardly counts because we saw a movie with seven other people and he didn't kiss me. He did hold my hand, though. I remember his palms were sweaty and clammy, and when he finally released my hand, I had to focus so hard on not wiping it on my jeans I missed the end of the movie. Then there was Trevor. Trevor's hands were always warm. Even in the dead of winter, when it was too cold to snow, his palms would be toasty. "It's just a biological necessity," he'd say. "To ensure you always need me to keep you warm."

Some instinct takes over and I pull away.

"What's wrong?" Astor asks.

"Nothing," I say, picking up my water glass. I take a small sip, keeping my eyes on the table.

"Caggie?" He sets his elbows on the table and leans forward.

"I don't know you," I say. I'm talking to my plate.

"But you could." I look up and he's staring at me again. I see something in his eyes I haven't seen in a long time. Something that reminds me of things I've been trying to forget. But what's strange is that it doesn't make me cower, like I expect it to. It makes me lean a little bit closer.

"Why me?" I ask.

He shakes his head slowly. He picks up his knife and threads it between two fingers. "I think we're alike. I told you that before." He sets the knife down, glances up at me.

The night Trevor broke up with me, we were in my room. We were trying to decide whether to watch a movie, order in, or go out to eat. Well, he was, anyway. I wasn't really paying attention. I was focused on what I was always focused on— this lump in my stomach, a stone sinking through water. I kept waiting for it to hit the bottom, but it never did.

He must have asked me what I wanted to do at least five times, but I don't remember. Finally he stood up. I could see he was annoyed, which was unusual for Trevor. Trevor could spend the entire day filing paperwork or doing the same math problem and not get bored. It's just his nature. But that night was different.

"This isn't working," he said.

"What?" I remember looking, stupidly, for some kind of appliance. I remember thinking maybe he was talking about the television or his cell phone.

"Us." He looked at me when he said it, and I could see how much the one word hurt him. More, maybe, than it even hurt me.

I stayed on the floor and pulled my legs up to my chest. "It's fine," I said. "I get it."

He shook his head. "You don't."

"Yes, I do. I'm not the same person I was before. You don't want to be with this girl. It's okay. I understand."

He sank down to his knees then. I thought maybe he was going to start praying. "I don't think you want me to help," he said. "I just think it might be easier for you if I wasn't here."

I wanted to tell him how wrong he was. That this wasn't about him helping; there was nothing he could do. He didn't understand that when your sister dies there isn't anything anyone can do. And I was mad at him. I was angry that it was his bracelet, his piece of protection, I kept seeing at the bottom of the pool. It was supposed to keep me safe, and instead it had killed her. It was at that moment, with him on his knees, that I understood something had been broken in me that was still whole in him. That I understood that we were nothing alike at all.

I blink and look at Astor. "It's just . . . my life for the last eight months has been pretty unrecognizable. It's hard to know what I am anymore."

"You're real," he says. "You're not a fake like those girls Abigail and Constance." He leans forward, stretches his fingertips across the table toward mine for a second time. "I just know. I could tell the moment I met you."

Something about the way he says the last word, "you," like it's chocolate on his tongue, like he's reveling in it, makes me take his hand. I want to believe him. To see what he sees in me. In fact, for the first time since January, I feel understood.

We stay that way, our fingers looped together over the linen tablecloth, for what feels like a long time. Time passes differently when really terrible things happen. It glides out, stops short, hurtles itself backward. It's hard to mark the moments. They don't follow any kind of linear trajectory. But sitting with Astor in that bistro downtown something shifts, like a tectonic plate clicking into place underneath us. Time stops entirely. I'm not trying to go back to before Hayley and I'm not trying to push forward, to figure out a way to "move on." I'm just here, now. I don't have to carry the same burden with Astor. I don't have to pretend I'm capable of anything I'm not.

He doesn't need me to be different.

CHAPTER SEVEN

"Be careful—it's Ming," my mother says as an assistant takes a vase down from the bookcase in our living room. *Vanity Fair* is here, and they're doing a piece on us for their "New York Royalty" issue. It will come out in three months.

We're taking a family portrait that will go next to the one of my grandfather that hangs above the mantel. My mother is micromanaging the situation, and my dad and Peter are in a corner, checking sports scores.

Hayley runs between my mother and Peter. She's refusing to change out of her dress—the white-and-blue one she calls her Alice in Wonderland. It has some paint splattered on it from this morning's activity, an imperfection our mother is refusing to overlook. She's not in a good mood—my uncle hasn't shown up.

My dad looks up from his phone just in time to catch Hayley as she saunters over. She seems to be showing off the paint stain like an award.

"Hi, baby," Dad says.

Hayley sticks her hands right on her hips. She knows what he's up to.

"You think you could do this one thing for your mother?" he asks, pointing to the crusted fuchsia marks.

Hayley has been screaming no at Mom, but for Dad she stops. I can see her thinking. So can Mom, but she pretends not to be listening.

"Okay," Hayley says. "But then we go to Sherman's."

Sherman's is her paint-supply store on Madison. My father holds up his hands in victory.

"Of course," he tells her. "Right after we take this picture."

She nods, and runs from the room. But then she turns back. She runs straight at my dad, gives him a kiss on the cheek.

"Knew that would cost me," he says when she's left.

"But worth it," I say.

My dad glances at my mom, who is back to business, refluffing throw pillows. He doesn't say it, but I can tell he's thinking the same thing.

*　*　*

I roll over in bed, the last remnants of dream memory dissolving into the morning sun streaming through my window. That afternoon, almost two years ago now. It was the start of so much. My parents have always been high in New York social circles—old money, etc.—but that *Vanity Fair* piece skyrocketed things. It made us seem like we were folklore, fantasy. It made us seem great. I remember Hayley coming home from school asking why people kept bugging her about Granddad. "Did he do something bad?" she asked.

I told her no, of course not, he was just a very talked-about man. Sometimes people said nice things, and sometimes they said things that weren't very kind at all. The truth is he was strict. He was severe. He didn't even stay married too long. He didn't really get along well with anyone.

Well, anyone besides me. He liked me. My mom said right away. Children weren't really his thing—he barely once picked Peter up—but it was different with me.

I remember hours spent on my father's study floor playing horsie with him, or reading bedtime stories at my uncle's house in California.

There was one trip when we were walking on the beach in Malibu, just Granddad and I. We would do that sometimes—

duck out of the house and have beach dates together.

I remember I bent to pick up a shell. It wasn't anything special. Just one of those white ones with the ridges that line any beach. It was whole, though. That part was unusual. I handed it to him and he gave it back to me. "You keep it," he said. Granddad put his arm around me then, and we faced toward the ocean. I don't remember how long we stood there, but it was a while. Long enough for me to watch a boat disappear out to sea. "You're really mine," he said. It was soft, but I heard him. "Your father never was, but you are."

I never felt like I fit with my family. Not my mom or my dad, not even Peter—he's way too self-assured. But Hayley was mine, just like I was my grandfather's.

Sometimes I still can't believe they are both gone.

I throw back the covers and head into the bathroom. I splash some water on my face, apply cream, change into my uniform. The kitchen is quiet. My mother is already gone. I see Peter's baseball cap on the kitchen table, METS stenciled across the top. I pick it up. I know he's not here—my mother was probably cleaning out some drawer or closet or something—but I still press it up against my chest before I set it back down. Like maybe there is a little of him in there. A little bit of some kind of home still stored inside the brim.

I keep my eyes trained off the family portrait—the one

that still hangs in our sitting room—as I leave for school. I know I'll see Hayley, front and center. Smiling wide, new dress on, hands on her hips. Alive.

"Hey, wait up."

I turn around to see Trevor jogging behind me. School has just ended, and I'm trying to hightail it home. Astor and I are going to see a movie tonight—something with sunflowers in the title, at the Angelika—and I want to change first. It's only been three days since our dinner, but I'm anxious to see him. Some time between classes at school hasn't really been much. Or enough.

"What?" I snap.

Trevor takes a step back. "You didn't show up yesterday."

"For what?" I ask. I blow some stray hair off my forehead.

He just keeps looking at me. "The first day of the *Journal*."

The *Journal* is a creative-writing magazine that Kensington funds and puts out. Getting to be a part of it is a big deal. It's actually published and available to the public, unlike the paper, that is just for us. Getting elected is this ridiculously rigorous process whereby you have to sign up and then be nominated and then go before a board and present your creative vision. Trevor and I got elected last year, way back in December. They plan early. I think we had the upper hand all along, though. It's pretty common knowledge that Mrs.

Lancaster, the faculty point person, has a crush on Trevor. She's in her sixties, probably, and she's always saying things to Trevor like "If I were a lifetime younger, you'd have to watch out."

Anyway, the *Journal* publishes students' writing pieces and some printed artwork, as well as general submissions. It's really well respected. Jonathan Franzen once had a piece published in it. A bunch of *New Yorker* contributors too. Being the school paper editor helped me, and Trevor and I landed ourselves the positions of coeditors along with a faculty member and a creative-writing professor from Columbia. We went out to our favorite diner, Big Daddy's, to celebrate after we found out. Trevor ordered us both chocolate shakes, and we sat in the booth for hours pouring over old copies of the *Journal* and talking about how we were going to change it once it was in our hands.

"I forgot," I say. "Sorry." I drop my hands down by my sides. I try not to look him in the eye.

Trevor folds his arms across his chest. His school blazer is off, and he's wearing a blue T-shirt, one I know well. It has a small ink stain at the bottom left corner, right by the seam, from the night I chewed through a pen studying for a calculus exam. When I asked him why he didn't throw it away, he told me he liked it even more now. "It has your mark on it," he said. "Just like I do."

Trevor shakes his head. "I covered for you, but they weren't happy. It's a big deal, Caggs."

"I'm aware," I say.

"Our next meeting is tomorrow," he says, taking a step closer to me. "Here." He hands me a piece of paper with a schedule on it. "That has all the information."

"Thanks."

"Sure." He opens his mouth again, like he's going to say something, but instead he just lets his arms swing to the side.

"I gotta go," I say. I take off before either one us has the chance to say good-bye.

Seeing Trevor, talking about the *Journal*, makes me want to get to Astor even faster. When he rings the doorbell an hour later, it feels like it's been a month.

"Miss me?" He's leaning against the door, and he's changed from school. He's now wearing a blue button-down and jeans, and I can tell he's showered from the way his hair looks—newly done. A tiny bit crunchy at the ends.

"I just saw you at school," I say. I keep my hands by my sides. I try not to let my impatience show, although I don't think I'm doing too good a job.

"Feels like forever."

I have a light feeling in my stomach, like champagne bubbles rising. "Do you want to go?" I ask.

He nods.

I slip my bag over my shoulder and close the door. He doesn't move to let me pass by, and I'm suddenly aware of him next to me. Of the way he smells—like expensive cologne, like Paris—and how it makes me want to move closer. How I want to put my hand around the back of his neck and pull him in.

He takes my hand.

"I thought we could walk a bit after," he says.

"After the movie? I should probably start my English paper—"

He swings me around. Fast. My words get lost on the way. "No," he says. "After this." He lets go of my hand and loops his arms around my waist. Then he draws me toward him and places a hand on my cheek. He runs his thumb there and then moves his lips over mine. We start kissing. I disentangle my arms from my sides, and then I'm grabbing at his hair, his neck, his shoulders—whatever I can reach. His hands reach around me, travel up my sides. His lips on mine feel hot, frantic. When we break apart, we're both breathing hard.

"Not bad," he whispers.

He leans his forehead to mine; I angle myself so I'm pressed against his chest.

It doesn't make sense. I barely know him. It shouldn't make me feel this good to be close to him. Like I want to slip underneath his shirt and breathe against his skin. But I do.

"Maybe we should skip the movie," he says, planting a kiss by my ear.

I lean back and look at him. Raise my eyebrows. "But what would we do?"

He smiles. So do I.

I take his hand and lead him back inside. Past the foyer, up the stairs, down the hallway, and into my room. But when we get inside, I'm actually not sure what to do. Trevor is the only guy besides Peter who has even been in my bedroom, and as soon as I open the door, I think maybe I've made a mistake bringing Astor here. I'm acutely aware of the voice in my head, the one that was silenced for a while by his kisses, the one that is now reminding me that I hardly know him.

"So, this is it," I say. I stand holding the doorknob, like at any moment I might need to bolt.

"It's nice," he says.

He picks up a glass figurine of a ballerina that's sitting on my desk. Something Claire bought me at an auction a few years ago. Some of her father's photos were being auctioned. Claire just liked raising her paddle, and eventually she won something. I kind of love it. It reminds me of her.

"Ballet?" He asks.

I shrug. "It was a gift."

"I see."

I wrap my arms around me. Something about the way he's prowling my room, like he's looking for clues, makes me feel exposed. There is a lot he could find out about me here.

He sets the ballerina down and comes over to me. "I like your room," he says.

He runs his eyes over my face. His gaze feels hot—I swear it might even burn me. And then he reaches forward and takes my face in his hands and starts kissing me again.

We end up on my bed. He slides his hands down my sides and underneath my shirt. They feel warm against my skin, and I reach up to pull him closer.

He holds my waist with his palms and then backs off a little—kissing my neck, my nose, the bridges of my eyebrows.

"You're too much," he says.

"Me?"

"Yes, you," he says. He props himself up on his elbow and runs a finger in a figure eight over my stomach. I shiver. "I didn't think I'd find you at Kensington."

"What did you think you'd find?" I ask.

He lifts his finger. Touches my shoulder. "Abigail, maybe."

I exaggerate a shudder. "You're pretty lucky, then."

"I'd say so."

He kisses me again.

"Tell me something," he says.

"Like what?"

"Something about yourself." He trails a flat palm down my arm.

"That's pretty broad."

He kisses my ear. "Try."

"I used to ride horses," I exhale.

He pulls back and looks at me. "Better than that."

"I never had braces?"

"I heard you saved a girl's life last year."

All at once his hands on me feel like ice blocks. My blood has frozen in my veins.

"Did I say something?" he asks.

I sit up, nudging him off me. "It's fine," I say.

He knits his eyebrows together. "Something tells me this isn't just you being modest."

I hug my knees to my chest. "There isn't anything to tell. People made a big deal about nothing. I don't like to dwell on it."

He nods but doesn't say anything.

"It happened and it's over and everything turned out okay. I don't see the point in talking about it."

"I think it's pretty cool," he says. He leans down so we're eye level.

"It's not a goal," I say. "She was just . . . there." The familiar guilt blooms in my stomach. Acid. Bile. It makes me want to vomit up the truth fast.

"Still," he says. "Saving someone . . . doesn't it make you feel like there is a reason for all of this?"

"All of what?"

"Life." He looks me square in the eye. "Tragedy."

In that moment I know he knows about Hayley. I've gotten good at spotting it. The way people's eyes twitch, like their pupils are dilating. The way they can't maintain eye contact for more than a moment or the way their body goes slack, like they're responding to the news themselves. It's easy to tell when people are thinking about Hayley.

"How do you—?"

"'The Caulfield granddaughter drowns. Life mirrors art. Allie and Hayley: the lost Caulfield children.'" He spouts out the headlines, the ones that graced the papers for two full weeks after she drowned.

"Right." I nod. I sit back against my headboard.

"It's okay," he says. "You don't have to talk about it. I just didn't want you to think you had to hide anything from me." He moves forward, cups my chin with his hand. "Cool?"

I shake my head yes. "Yeah," I say.

"Hey." He doesn't remove his hand. "Look at me." I glance up, and his gaze holds mine. "You don't have to talk about it. You don't have to talk about anything."

People have told me so many times that I don't have to talk about it. Friends, neighbors, teachers. They're always saying, "You don't have to talk about it if you don't want to." But what they really mean is *I expect you to answer all my questions. I expect you to cry. I expect you to show me the way you feel.* Astor is the first person that when he says it, I believe him. Something in the way his eyes look into mine makes me know he's not going to push me on it. It makes me relax against him. Into him.

He kisses me again, and then he lies down next to me, so we're both staring up at the ceiling.

"I used to think I understood life. That I sort of had it figured out." He turns his head to look at me. "Do you know what I mean?"

I nod. "Yeah. But then everything—"

"Fell apart."

I exhale. "That's how it goes. One minute you're aboveground and the next you're under."

"I'm sorry," he says. I feel him take my hand.

My phone rings. I groan and roll to my side, snatching up my bag. I bounce out my phone. It's Claire, calling from home. I look at Astor propped up on one elbow on my bed, his blue button-down barely crinkled. Claire would understand, I think. I hit ignore and roll back toward him.

"I like that," he says.

He sits up and starts kissing me again. I kiss him back. I move myself closer to him, and he reaches up and snaps me against his chest. I let my head fall to the side and feel him start kissing my collarbone, then up to my neck, then—

My cell phone rings again. I lurch back, but Astor is still working on my ear. "What's wrong?" he murmurs.

I move off him and snatch up my phone from the floor. Claire again. I silence it once more, but this time I feel bad about it. She's pretty persistent, and it has never been an emergency. Claire once called me four times in a row, and when I finally got out of the shower and called her back, she just wanted to tell me she had found her first split end. But I still feel bad. I don't usually screen her calls.

"You should go," I say.

We're not touching anymore, but I can feel him next to me. Like the air between us is charged—that thick, unstable space right before magnets lock.

"My mom'll be home any minute, and I really should return that," I say, but I make no solid effort to stand. To get off the bed. It's like there are two opposing forces inside me—one I've been fighting for a long, long time and one I just learned was there. I'm not sure which to listen to.

He gets up first. "Okay. Can I see you tomorrow?"

"Yes."

He leans down, touches my arm. "Other than at school."

"I know what you mean."

I watch him leave from the spot on my bed. I don't get up

to walk him to the door. I don't move at all. When he's closed it behind him, I lie back down. I curl up into a ball, on my side. I shut my eyes.

There it is again. Our beach house. The pool. Kristen on the rooftop. If I could empty my mind out, shake it onto the floor and let the memories fall like pennies from a piggy bank, I would. But I can't. Instead I try to replace them. I think about Astor here, just a moment ago. About his lips on mine. His hands on my back. About his black eyes and cool palms and the weight of his gaze.

CHAPTER EIGHT

The next day I drag my feet to the *Journal* offices after school. It's the same office that runs the school paper—a small computer lab on the second floor of our main building. The walls are covered in bulletin boards that have news clippings and short stories from the *Journal* that have won awards. I put most of those up there. Me and Trevor, anyway. I couldn't possibly count how many hours we've spent in here over the last two years. There were plenty of nights Trevor and I would stay so late that we'd have to lock up the main school building. We'd order in greasy Chinese or Thai and work off side-by-side computers. Claire would stop by postdate and fill us in on whatever artist or billionaire's son she was currently seeing.

Sometimes we'd do dramatic readings of particularly bad student submissions. The best was this one time Constance submitted a poem. It was under a pseudonym, but she printed it on her own letterhead—she must have forgotten when she turned it in. The poem was titled "Sunday," and it was clearly about Tripp. She didn't even bother to change his name much. The repeating line went like this:

Troy, you're my best friend's boy.

Trevor sang it like a really bad pop song, and I remember looking at him and thinking, *God, I seriously love this kid.*

"I don't know," Trevor said when he finished. "I think we should print it."

"Funny," I said.

"I'm serious. I think we'd be doing Troy a really big favor." He smiled, leaned down over me. I was sitting in a swivel chair, my feet tucked up, turning side to side. He put his hands on the arms of the chair and stopped me from moving. Then he leaned down and kissed me.

Kissing Trevor was pretty epic. You know the moment in the movies when the music swells, right near the end? Kissing Trevor was like the end of a movie. Every single time.

"I bet Abigail wouldn't even notice if we printed it with Constance's name on it," I said when he pulled back.

"Troy could also mean Trevor, you know."

"Do you wish you were Constance's boy?" I asked, running my hands through his hair.

"Desperately," he said, kissing me again. "The only reason I date you is to get close to her."

"I figured."

"She's pretty hot," he said.

"Yeah?" I asked, bringing my lips up to meet his.

"Mm-hmm," he whispered. "She's cute. And sexy. And she's got these little freckles right below her ear." He lifted my hair then, and kissed me on the neck.

"Constance doesn't have freckles," I corrected. "She spray tans."

Trevor slapped the back of his hand against his forehead. "That's right. I must have been thinking about you." He brought his lips so they hovered right above mine. "Funny how that always seems to happen."

"You're going to the *Journal*?" Claire says. She called as I climbed the stairs, and I picked up, despite the fact that I'm already late. I still feel bad about silencing her yesterday and then not calling her back.

"Yes," I say. I can tell she's smiling. Claire is pretty easy to read, if you want to know the truth. "Just trying to make you happy," I say.

Claire scoffs. "I never told you to go back to the *Journal*."

"You've been pushing me out of pajamas all summer," I say. "Turns out you have to get dressed for this activity, so I thought you'd approve."

"True," she says. "You know what? I will take full responsibility for your emotional progress."

Emotional progress. I open my mouth to tell Claire about Astor, but something stops me. I don't know why. She'd be thrilled, I think. She was the one who pushed me toward him in the first place.

"Shocking," I say. "But I gotta go."

"You're so busy lately," she says. "I never see you."

"So come uptown."

"You know I don't go above Fourteenth Street anymore," she says. Going above Fourteenth Street isn't actually hard to do, but since Claire moved downtown, she's really embraced the lifestyle. There is silence on the other end of the phone for a moment. "Have you seen Kristen?" she asks.

It makes me stop on the steps. "She goes here," I say.

"Right," she says. "Yeah. I was just wondering how she was doing."

"She's fine," I say. The words have to fight through my teeth. I picture Kristen in class, her tiny frame, small voice. And she is fine, right? She's fine. My stomach just keeps tightening. My brain immediately starts the familiar tirade: *You were wrong. You were weak. You ruined someone's life just so you wouldn't have to fess up to what a failure you have become. What a phony.*

I hear Claire exhale. "Okay," she says. "I miss you. Don't forget who was here first."

We hang up before I can tell her what I want to—that she was here first until she left, which isn't my fault. I open the *Journal* office door to find everyone already there, sitting in a small circle. Mrs. Lancaster, Whitney Davon—a Columbia professor—and Trevor. He smiles when he sees me, and I can tell it's one of relief. I showed. He's got his Kensington blazer off again, and one of his cotton T-shirts stretches against his chest. I feel my face heat up. I look away. Try to shake the cold voice from my head.

"Good of you to join us, Mcalister." Mrs. Lancaster makes a point of tapping her watch.

I don't say anything, just nod.

"Please take a seat," she says, motioning to an empty chair. It's the one closest to the door, thank God.

As soon as I'm seated, Trevor jumps in. "Caggie and I have a lot of great ideas for this year."

Mrs. Lancaster eyes Trevor with wide fascination. So does Whitney. Whitney is pretty, probably late twenties. I forgot the effect Trevor has on girls, women, people of all ages, really. When we were together I stopped noticing. I knew he was in it with me, so what did it matter? I didn't have to worry.

"We really think this year is the one to take things to the next level," Trevor says. His eyes are hopeful, bright. They look right at me.

"Mcalister, why don't you elaborate?" Mrs. Lancaster sets her notebook down on a stray desk.

I know we had ideas, lots of them. We wanted to have a "first lines" competition among the students. We had a list of writers who were willing to contribute pieces. We wanted to do reverse interviews where novelists interviewed students, instead of the other way around. I came up with that. When I think about that now, sitting here in this lopsided circle, it feels like it was someone else. How could I have cared about any of this? How did it ever seem important?

We had a lot of plans. But I had a lot of plans about a lot of things. Those didn't work out too well, and sitting in this room, I know I can't work with Trevor. The thought of us collaborating on something, anything, feels fake. Like I'd be pretending things are the same, when they're not.

I shrug. "I don't remember, really. Maybe Trevor does." I can feel Trevor gaping at me, but I don't look at him. I just cross my arms and stare out the window. It's eye level with the sky. All I see are buildings.

Mrs. Lancaster clears her throat. "Trevor, do you have something to add?"

I can feel Trevor's gaze on me, the questions in his eyes. Let him wonder. That's all I did this summer: wonder. Wonder where he was, what he was doing. Why he left. And then all of a sudden I can't take being here anymore. I need to get out.

"Big test tomorrow," I lie. "I'll work on some stuff for Monday." I know I won't. I won't come back. Even the *Journal*, the thing that was supposed to make senior year, the thing that I was most excited about, can't provoke a reaction. There is no going back. Not to Trevor, not to the things I cared about before. Not to anything.

I leave and call Astor from the hallway. "Hey," he says when he picks up. "I was hoping it would be you."

"Are you free?"

"Are you kidding?"

I feel that familiar fluttering in my chest. "You weren't at school."

I hear Astor laugh. "My day's just getting started."

"Do you want to come over?"

"Yes."

"I'll be home in fifteen."

I hang up and glance back at the door to the *Journal* room. I imagine Trevor looking at my empty chair. Whitney's eye on him. I picture him making some excuse for me, for why I left in such a hurry. I don't feel bad that he's getting a turn to lie.

CHAPTER NINE

The strange thing about missing someone is that sometimes it pushes you in the opposite direction, straight away from them. After the day at the *Journal*, Trevor and I barely speak, and Astor and I start seeing each other all the time. Every free moment. We spend lunches together at Kensington—lying out on the grass in the park, sitting on the benches on Fifth, even pushing our chairs together in the corner of the library, skipping class and hiding out. I get college applications in the mail and I stuff them in a drawer. How can I possibly choose a future when I am so focused on getting through the present?

I tell Claire about Astor the day after the *Journal*.

"This is excellent news," she says. "Now maybe you'll stop hibernating."

But the opposite turns out to be true. Summer turns to fall in New York, but for Astor and me it may as well be winter.

I see Claire less. I stop studying. I don't seem to care about anything but being with him. I dream about how it feels to be close to him. How it makes the rest of my life delete down to nothing.

Even Hayley lessens. The pain is dissolving, just a little. When I'm with Astor, it's harder to remember.

And he doesn't make me. He just tells me he understands, and if I don't want to talk about it, that is okay. He doesn't try to hold me the way Trevor used to. He doesn't tell me that I could say anything to him and he'd still be there. It's okay if I say nothing.

"Do you ever think about dying?" Astor asks me a month later. October is creeping in on tiptoes.

We're supposed to be studying in my room, but I haven't cracked the pages of a single book yet. We're lying on the floor, my head resting on his stomach. It rises and falls with an irregular beat, like jazz music, every time he talks.

I pick up his arm where it stretches next to me and hug it to my chest. "Not right now," I say. "Why?"

He shrugs. My head rocks on his stomach. "Sometimes I think about it."

I sit up and look at him. "I try not to."

He sighs and sits up, too. "Don't you ever wonder what happened to them?"

"Them?"

He shakes his head. "Hayley."

I inhale. My head feels light. "She died," I say. "That's what happened to her."

"But where did she go?"

I make a move to stand. "Why are you asking me this?" The past has invaded our little bubble. I can almost hear it pop.

He reaches for my hand. "Are you pissed at me?"

I shake my head. "I don't want to ruminate on death. It's not romantic."

"Hey." He gathers me up into his lap. I let him. "That's not at all what I mean. I was just curious."

I look into his eyes. They make me want to fall inside, find another world there.

"I'm curious about things too," I say softly.

Astor doesn't talk about his past. It's like an unspoken rule we have: Don't ask, don't tell. But I know something happened. I can feel it. Something besides getting kicked out of school. Something bigger. Opaque. He's never said what it is, and I haven't pushed. After all, I know what that's like, and how much I hate it. To be totally honest, I'm not so sure I want to know.

I get these hints of things, like echoes that have lost the word they once were. That have become just sound. When he talks, I know there is something behind what he's saying. But he never expands on it. And I haven't figured it out on my own, either. I haven't been to his house; I haven't met his parents. I haven't wanted to. I think maybe this is better. Maybe this is how it should be. I knew everything about Trevor, and look where that got me. Astor and I get the opportunity to start over. With him I can be anyone.

"Come on," he says. He slides a firm, flattened palm down my back. "I'm sorry I brought it up. Really."

The moment takes over, the way it always does, and in the next instant the past is far away.

Things escalate quickly. This has been happening a lot lately. We end up on my bed. His hands slip under my shirt and start exploring. He runs his thumb down my side, kisses my collarbone.

Trevor and I had sex after our winter formal last year. December fifteenth. It's weird to remember a date like that, like an anniversary or something, even though we aren't still together. I initiated it. We had talked about it a lot. Whether we were ready. How we wanted our first time to be together. That kind of thing. Trevor wasn't pushy. If we were kissing or something, he'd always slow things down. He said it was my decision to make, mine alone. What he didn't understand was that I wanted to. I had wanted to from the first few months we'd started dating. But everything was so complicated with Trevor. There was so much involved there, so much that sex meant to both of us. Everything had so much more weight back then—what we thought sex stood for to us, to our relationship. It was indulgent. Naïve. It was so stupid to think that things like that mattered. That they made any impact on my life at all.

Trevor brought me to the Waldorf Astoria. I pretended I was mad at him for spending so much money, but secretly I was thrilled. I knew he had been saving up his tutoring money for weeks for this—months, probably. We were quiet in the elevator up to the fifteenth floor, but when the doors opened, he scooped me up. He carried me all the way down the hallway. When we got to the room he tried to take the key out of his pocket, but couldn't with me in his arms.

"Can you get that?" he asked me.

I pulled it out and he angled me toward the door. The green light flickered and I opened it.

He was still carrying me when I saw the rose petals lining the way from the door to the bed. There were candles lit too, and a bottle of sparkling apple cider on ice.

"I wanted it to be special," he whispered.

I'm really embarrassed to admit this, but I teared up. I buried my head in his chest and he wrapped his arms tighter around me. He didn't move, didn't put me down; he just held me. Then he placed me on the bed. I remember thinking it was strange. We'd been alone together so many times—hundreds—but everything felt so new, so foreign, like we were strangers.

Until he started kissing me. There were no two ways around it. Kissing Trevor was just . . . home.

"I can't," I breathe. Astor keeps kissing me until I reach up and gently push his shoulders away.

"What's wrong?" he asks. His voice is hoarse.

I sit back and shake my head. "I don't know, I just can't."

The truth is that sleeping with him scares me. Not the actual sex, I don't think. Trevor and I only did it a handful of times more after December fifteenth, so I'm not an expert or anything, but I do know what to expect. It's more that being with Astor feels unknown. Intense. Like it might make me feel too much.

"Let's go out," I say.

Astor slides himself up onto one elbow. "Where?"

"We could go downtown and meet Claire."

He runs his outstretched palm over my comforter, traces a stitched flower there. "I don't think she likes me very much," he says.

"That's ridiculous!" I say it a little too loudly. "You guys have never even hung out before."

"But I keep you away from her."

Okay, so I haven't been around as much the last month, but Claire has disappeared for guys plenty of times. She got defensive about it last week. She tried to tell me she didn't think I was being "myself." That I had "dropped off." What she doesn't understand is that for the first time in eight months I actually feel like I'm surviving. That I'm not lying on the floor broken into a million pieces. I think she's just annoyed she wasn't the one to put me back together.

"Come on," I say, tugging him off the bed. "I'll call her."

"Is it really you?" she says when she picks up. I can hear the sarcasm in her voice, and for a moment it makes me angry. She's so obvious—she can't even pretend to be happy for me. Why should I feel bad for spending time with Astor? I've never given her grief about any of the guys she's been with.

"The one and only," I say. Astor and I are sitting on my floor, and he's flipping through a *New Yorker* magazine, his legs crossed beneath him.

"You should see my last call logged from you. Somewhere in the vicinity of two weeks ago," Claire says. I hear the clank of the freezer door opening. Ice cube trays rattle.

"I could hang up and call you again, if you're looking for frequency?"

The background noise goes quiet, and I can almost hear

her smile. "Yuk yuk," she says. "So what's going on?"

Astor flips a page and looks up. He reaches over and tucks some hair behind my ear. Instinctively, I move the phone away. "Oh, you know, the usual. School, blah blah," I say.

"Hey, want to get dinner?" Claire asks. "There's this show on the Bowery we could check out too."

"Dinner sounds good. Where should we meet you?"

There's a pause on the other end, and I know she's responding to the word "we." It makes something inside me flare up again. Claire never used to care when we hung out with Trevor. She'd sometimes say she preferred his company to mine. I knew she was joking, but it was just never an issue. I don't know why she's being so intolerant of Astor.

"How does Eataly sound?" she says. The attitude is gone from her voice, and I know she's working hard at it. "We can sit up on the roof, have some salads or something?"

Eataly is one of my favorite spots in the city. It's an Italian food market with a restaurant on the roof that has great city views. Claire always calls it a tourist trap, and she's right, but there is something I still really love about it. It's so crowded it's almost possible to disappear. Usually I have to con her into setting foot in that place. I know this is her peace offering, and my anger dissolves. I swallow the last remnants like the grainy bits of juice at the bottom of a glass.

"Sure," I say. "Sounds great."

After I hang up, Astor places a hand on my stomach. He casually flips one of the buttons of my shirt open.

"Hey," I say. I slap his hand away playfully. "We just made plans."

He reaches back. Flips another one. "Just give me a few minutes."

I sit up, pull my shirt closed. "Now." I raise my eyebrows.

"She's waited, in her words, weeks. What's another five minutes?" He bends his lips to my neck, and I press his head back up.

"That's not exactly how it works."

He's still trying for my neck, and his words come out light and playful. "So tell me, then. How does it work?"

"Do you want her to like you? Then we should be on time." I push myself off the floor.

"I was just trying to see you for a minute," he says, grabbing for his loafer. "This doesn't need to be some dramatic scene."

"I'm not making a scene," I say, crossing my arms. I feel small, indignant—like a child refusing a bedtime or dinner.

"Sure seems like it." His tone has changed. He's annoyed, and his words have a clipped edge to them. It's a side of him I haven't seen before. I don't like it.

"I'm sorry," I say. I can feel my voice breaking. I just want to get out of here. He sighs, runs a hand over his chin. Then he turns to me. "No, I'm sorry." He comes over to where I'm standing and puts his arms around my waist. "I guess some-times I don't want to share you."

"Claire is my friend," I say.

"So let's go be with her." He steps in front of me and opens the door. I go to follow him and then stop. There are still some books in my bag, and they're weighing it down. I take them out and place them on my desk. When I look up, I catch that picture of Trevor and me. Winter formal. I pick it up.

Astor turns around and looks at the photo in my hands. My heart seems to stop.

"What's that?" he asks.

"Nothing," I say quickly. Too quickly.

He lifts the picture up. My pulse fires through my veins.

"You guys were together, right? You and Trevor?"

I nod. I keep my head low. Plenty of people have ex-boyfriends. It's not a crime. But the past has crept in, some-how. Even though we've tried to keep it out, here it is.

I blink and look at him. "We broke up in May."

"Okay."

I keep on. "I've had the entire summer to get over it." I hug my arms to my chest.

Astor puts the picture down and takes my hand in his. His touch feels like a weight being lifted.

"I don't even know why I still have that picture there," I say. "Are you mad?"

"No," he says. "I'm not." He keeps his gaze fixed on mine. I'm not sure if I believe him.

"Trevor doesn't have anything to do with my life now," I say.

Astor nods. "I know," he says finally.

"I just don't want you to think that . . ." I hate myself for talking like this, for the slightly pleading edge to my tone. But I don't want to lose any part of him—not his trust, not anything. I can't.

He tucks me to him and his face is recognizable again. Softer. "I know," he says again.

There is something new between us now, something charged. The past is here, but it's not a dead weight—not like it was with Trevor. It's not something I have to carry around with me, then unpack and explain. It's something fluid, like mercury. It coils and spills. It travels. Infects. Astor is a part of this too now. And I can't help but feel grateful for that.

Eataly is across from Madison Square Park on Fifth Avenue. Above Fourteenth, so it's a surprise Claire suggested it. It doesn't take us too long to get downtown; traffic is oddly light for this time of weekday evening.

Claire is hanging out by the hostess stand when we get there. She's impossible to miss, and when I catch sight of her mile-high legs, something unhinges in me. I have the urge to run over to her and bury my head in her shoulder. But I don't. Maybe it's Astor, I'm not sure. But something stops me.

Claire has on a white button-down shirt that looks like a man's. In fact it is a man's. I know because my brother has the same one. It's thin, white cotton, with blue pinstripes and the Ralph Lauren logo on the breast pocket. It's not summer anymore, and I see a brown leather jacket tucked over her bag. Black Ray-Bans sit perched on her head, and she's thumbing through a magazine. *Vogue*, probably, but I can't see the front.

She looks up at us. I see her give Astor a once-over, slowly, before she turns to me. "They said ten minutes," she says. She folds the magazine into her bag and gives me a quick hug with the other arm. "Hey, Astor," she says over my shoulder. "Thanks for letting her come up for air."

I can't see his facial expression, but I hear him snort behind me.

"Where's Band Guy?" I ask when she releases me.

"Who?"

"Max?" I try. "Brooklyn?" I gesture toward Astor, and Claire's eyes get wide.

"Oh, him? Please. Done." She smacks her hands together. "He sent me this love poem that it turned out he stole off a blog. It was super creepy. I kept googling lines and they'd pop up on people's old Myspace pages. We broke up."

"I didn't really think that was a match," I confess. I knew it wouldn't last, it never does, but she did seem into him.

"I know," she says. "You may think differently, but you're a terrible liar."

Something in my stomach tightens. I'm still feeling a little shook-up from the picture incident in my room. "So who's in the mix now?" I ask, clearing my throat.

She tugs on her collar and shrugs. "No one."

"Yeah, right," I tease. "There is never no one."

"I'm not seeing anyone, okay?" She sighs and flips the call box in her hands. It's just lit up. Our table is ready.

We head into the elevator, then up the steps to the roof. There's a great view up here, one that makes you feel like you're a part of the Manhattan skyline. Like you're floating up in it, right along with the Chrysler Building. It's one of those views that makes me remember I live in New York. Trevor and I used to go for drinks at the Mandarin Oriental at Columbus Circle sometimes. There is a spectacular view of the park at the bar on the thirty-fifth floor. We'd put the ridiculously expensive drinks on my dad's tab and hole up in one of the couches by the windows. I liked looking at the city that way, from a distance. Like it was a painting, or a statue. Something composed, steadfast, fixed. Something eternal. Sometimes it's hard to tell what I miss more: what New York used to mean to me, or what Trevor did. They were so tied together. Trevor was my New York.

I squeeze Astor's hand. He squeezes back.

Claire orders champagne, and the waitress gives her a funny look. "You know what? Just bring me a Diet Coke," she says. Usually Claire wouldn't change her order, and if anyone gave her heat about it, she'd just call the owner, who inevitably knows her father. Even if they call to let him know, he doesn't care. Claire's dad has always had a pretty liberal view of drinking. Claire's been having wine at dinner with her family since she was like eleven.

"Cool place," Astor says, leaning back in his chair and surveying the scene. "You come here often?"

Claire shrugs. "I go everywhere often."

I roll my eyes and attempt to shove her under the table. "So how's school going?" I ask.

She takes a long sip of her drink. "Fine, I guess. Downtown kids are strange, but what else is new." She eyes Astor. "Where are you from, anyway?"

"Here."

She squints at him. "What were you doing in London, then?" Claire looks at me, perhaps to fill in.

Did I tell her he was in London? How does she know? And then: Do I even know what he was doing there? I think his dad moved over for business, but I'm not sure. I know he got kicked out of school, but I don't know why they moved over to begin with. There's a lot we haven't asked, because there's a lot we both don't want to talk about. Astor makes it easy to try to forget. To move on. I think, although I'm not sure about what, that I help him do the same.

I look down at the table, avoiding Claire's gaze. I don't say anything. I suddenly feel really self-conscious, like someone has walked in on me changing, my shirt tangled around my head, my arms trying to thrust through the sleeves.

I swallow, focus on my plate. "You moved over there, right?" I offer lamely.

Astor puts a hand on the back of my chair. He shrugs. "Sure. Yeah. Hey, what's good here?"

Claire frowns. "The cheese plate, gnocchi, and vegetable salad are all awesome," she says to him, her eyes on me.

I look over at him. He catches my eye and seems to read something there—worry, maybe. He reaches his hand to my shoulder and squeezes. "My dad had some business abroad. We moved over, and then when he left, it was easier for me to stay on." He cups my shoulder with his hand, traces the bones with his thumb. "Does that answer your question?"

I nod. "Of course," I say. "Right." I look across at Claire as if to say, *See, told you so,* but she has her eyes on the menu. I'm so annoyed at her for bringing this up. I know who Astor is. I know how he makes me feel—like things are finally okay. That's the important stuff. Who cares why he went to London? After all the countless dates I've listened to of hers, all the stupid decisions she's made, she can't even give me this. Hate starts to creep in, right along with anger. I'm livid at her for insinuating that I should doubt him.

We order, and the conversation shifts to Kensington. Claire wants to know the latest gossip—whether Abigail is still terrorizing me this year (yes, with her "friendship"), who Constance is dating (everyone), and whether or not Jack Fisher is back (yes, and yes, he's still gorgeous). I glance at Astor when I confirm, but he doesn't seem to mind. He just winks. "Hey, don't look at me," he says. "That guy's a stud."

Then Claire asks about Kristen.

"Why do you keep asking me this?" I snap back. My anger hasn't dissipated, and it all comes out in that one question.

Claire frowns, and her voice is quiet when she speaks. "I'm just trying to see how things are for you."

"She didn't end up in a mental hospital this summer, if that's what you're driving at." My words sound like they're laced with venom. I can taste it as they come out. Tangy and acidic.

Claire looks like I just socked her in the face. "What's your problem?" she asks. Claire isn't the kind of person to care whether or not Astor is sitting right here. She doesn't care about what's appropriate, or about doing things in private. If she wants to get into something, she will.

I glance at Astor. He's watching us with a quiet fascination. His expression is mild, but interested. Hard to read.

I exhale, turning my attention back to Claire. "I honestly don't really know. As you may recall, we were never friends."

Claire arches her eyebrows. "You're being weird about this."

"I'm not being weird," I explain. "I don't know what you want me to say."

Claire puts her elbows on the table and leans forward. She squints and looks at me, the way she does when she knows I'm lying, the way she did last year when she asked me, after the fact, whether Trevor and I had slept together. I wasn't ready to tell her yet, but she still pushed me anyway. She has no idea how to mind her own business. "This *is* my business," I remember her saying. But she was wrong then. And she's wrong about this, too. It's my life, not hers. All of a sudden I'm so sick of her. I'm so sick of her butting in and the way she always feels entitled to everything about my life. But she can't share this. She didn't lose a sister. She didn't lose Trevor. The fact that she thinks she can empathize, that she thinks she has any idea what it feels like to be me, is maddening.

"This looks great!" Astor says. He smiles as the waitress sets down our food. I can feel the tension across the table between me and Claire. It's palpable. Like thick fog—something you can see.

Finally Claire speaks. "My dad is going to Africa for a shoot next month," she says. She leans back in her chair to let the waitress set her pasta down. She gives me a look like *This isn't over,* but for the time being, we're moving on. "He asked me to go with him."

This time Astor jumps in. "You should. It's an incredible place."

"You've been?" I ask.

He nods. "Yeah, a while ago. I went with my dad. It's crazy there."

"What part?" she asks. "I think they're going to Tanzania."

Astor interlaces his fingers and stretches. "Southern. We did a safari and then a few days in Cape Town on our own."

"How long ago?"

He pauses. "Two years?"

Claire sits back in her chair. "Cool," she says. "Well, maybe I can hit you up for some info, then."

Astor holds out his hands. "Anytime," he says.

This should get her off my back. So we won't be the three musketeers like Trevor and I were with Claire, but he's trying, isn't he? That has to count for something.

Astor refuses to let us pay. Claire fights him for just a moment before thanking him. Another point in his favor, I hope. Although I'm becoming increasingly uncertain as to whether or not I care. Then we push back our chairs and take the elevator down to the street. Astor steps out onto the curb to hail us a cab, and Claire grabs my arm, dragging me over to the left.

"What's his deal?" she hisses. It's loud out on the street—wind, taxis, conversations—so I know he can't hear us. But I still can't believe she's doing this here.

"What are you talking about?" I ask. I shake myself loose from her grip. "He was perfectly nice to you."

"Why is he so guarded?" she says.

"What do you want from him? The story of his life? If you're so concerned, ask. I don't care. I know who he is *now*, that's enough for me."

Claire snorts. "You're so naïve."

"You're so shortsighted," I say. "You think that just because I don't make someone spill his soul to me after a week that he's not a real boyfriend. Not everyone is like you, Claire. Not everyone is just looking for a month."

Claire ignores the last part. "Boyfriend?" She looks at me; her eyes seem to expand in their sockets.

The word surprised me, too, but I don't take it back. Astor and I haven't officially discussed that, but I'm sure he is. He's got to be. I cross my arms. "I have never once put up a fight with you. Do you know how many losers you've dated?

How many pathetic dates I've listened in on? Astor's actually a really great guy, if you'd just get to know him."

"Do you?"

"What?"

She looks at me. Hard. "Know him, Caggs." She runs her fingers over her temple. "I'm just saying, you guys seem really close for two people who don't have the details down."

I square my shoulders. I think about that conversation in my bedroom. About Astor asking and then telling me it was okay not to talk. Claire's never made it okay not to talk. No wonder I never want to tell her anything.

I inhale. My tone is measured, even, when I speak. "Unlike you," I say, "Astor doesn't make me dwell on last year. I'm actually with someone who lets me move on. If I was still around you and Trevor, I'd be in the fetal position forever."

Claire shakes her head. I can see the hurt in her eyes, but she's good at masking it. "I'm worried about you," she says.

"All you wanted was for me to meet someone," I counter. "You were worried about me when I wasn't moving on; now you're worried about me that I have?"

"But that's just it," Claire says. "Whatever this is, it isn't moving on."

I open my mouth to ask her how the hell she knows that, but Astor has gotten a taxi.

"Oi!" he yells. He's holding the door open with one hand and waving me over with the other.

"I can't talk about this anymore," I say to Claire.

It's hard to tell, because she turns her head, her words coming out the side of her mouth like water out of a broken faucet. But I think I hear her say, "Me either," before she takes off back downtown.

CHAPTER TEN

You probably won't believe me, at this point, given what I've told you about my family, but before Hayley died, we used to have family dinners. Not every night, but when we could, when my dad was in town. Me, Mom, Dad, Peter, and Hayley. Trevor came a lot too. His mom is a nurse and works nights, so he'd come over after school and just kind of stay. We'd do homework in my room. Hayley would usually join in. She liked to hang out with us. Well, she liked to hang out with Trevor.

He was so good with her. I remember one afternoon last December we were all in my room. I had a final English paper due. Something on Edith Wharton that Trevor had already finished. He and Hayley were sketching on her big notepad on the floor. I was sitting at my desk. I kept hearing them laugh and whisper behind me.

"Can you guys keep it down?" I teased, turning around. "I'm trying not to fail out of school here."

"A B isn't failing, Caggs," Trevor said. "Sorry to disappoint."

I rolled my eyes at him and Hayley laughed. "You think we should tell her?" Hayley asked.

Trevor squinted at Hayley. "You think she can handle it?"

Hayley nodded enthusiastically. She started bouncing on the floor.

Trevor exaggerated an exhale. "I don't know. I'm just not sure. Have we thought this through enough?"

"She can!" Hayley cried. "I promise, she can! Let's tell her!"

Trevor nodded. "If you insist, Ms. Caulfield."

Hayley's eyes looked like saucers. They got like that—big and bright—when she was really excited about something.

Trevor cleared his throat. "Show her," he said.

Hayley held up the sketch pad they had been working on. "Congratulations!" was written on it in block letters, colored in purple and orange, her favorite colors.

I looked from Trevor to Hayley. Both of them were beaming. "Congratulations?"

Hayley looked like she was about to burst. "You and Trevor got the *Journal*!" She looked at Trevor and bit her lip. He started laughing.

"Is she serious?" I asked him.

Trevor nodded. "Yeah," he said. "It's ours."

I flew out of my chair and into his arms. I remember he picked me up and spun me around. Hayley clapped her hands together from the floor. Then he kissed me. One of his end-of-movie kisses. I didn't even care that Hayley was there. I wrapped my arms around his neck and let my toes leave the ground. "We get to spend all of next year together," he said, pulling back just a bit.

I touched my forehead to his. "We were going to do that anyway."

"Let's celebrate!" Hayley said.

I blew some air out of my lips. "I have to finish this paper."

Trevor set me down. "No problem," he said. "You work; we'll get the ice cream."

Hayley stood up and marched toward the door. "Chocolate?"

"You know it."

She smiled and disappeared into the hallway. Trevor pulled me to him. I wrapped my arms around his neck.

"I can't believe this," I said. "We seriously got it?"

"Seriously."

I threaded my fingers through his hair. "We're going to rock that thing."

"I know," he said. He cupped my face in his hands. Brought

his lips down to mine. We kissed for a few moments—the lazy kisses of two people who assume they have forever.

Then Hayley yelled from the hallway: "Trevor!"

He pulled back. "Her Majesty calls," he said.

I held on to his hand as we broke apart. "Trevor?" I said.

"Yeah?"

"Thank you."

He shook his head. "I didn't do anything," he said.

He followed Hayley out into the hallway then, but I remember thinking how wrong he was. He did everything. He was the one who took care of my sister. He was the one who loved me. Being with Trevor was like being wrapped in a warm sweater all the time. The way it felt to fold into him—it was a perfect fit. I didn't know then, of course, that that safety would start to act like a barrier. It was this space we'd created—this warm place—that became totally uninhabitable. We couldn't be there together anymore, so Trevor decided we shouldn't be together at all.

At dinner that night Trevor and I laid out our plans for the *Journal* to my parents. Hayley took notes at the table. About a week later I found an envelope under my door. Inside were two pieces of lined paper with *Submission for the* Journal *by Hayley Caulfield* scrawled across the top. There was a poem in Hayley's handwriting titled "My Sister Is the Best Friend."

Would Hayley still think that now? Would she know how

deeply I let her down? Do the dead hold grudges? Please, Hayley. Forgive me.

Peter comes home that Thursday. It's his third trip in two months. "I needed to do laundry," he jokes when I come into the kitchen in the morning and find him in front of the refrigerator.

"Flying cross-country seems a little excessive, even for you." I go over and hug him. "You seeing Felicia?"

Peter eyes me. "Nah, that's not really . . . She's away for the weekend."

"Are things okay with you guys?"

"We kinda broke up." He cocks his head to the side and smiles.

"Oh, man, Pete, I'm sorry." I put a hand on his shoulder.

"It's fine," he says. "It was for the best."

"Too many cute California girls?"

Peter laughs. "Something like that."

"So why are you back?" I slide onto a stool at the counter.

"I thought we could hang, kid."

"You flew three thousand miles to spend thirty-six hours with your little sister? What's going on, Pete?" But as soon as I say it, I know. I'm impressed by how quickly this plan took action. Three days, not bad. "I can't believe she called you." I say. Claire and I haven't spoken since Eataly, but I guess that doesn't mean she's been out of touch with all Caulfields.

Peter closes the glass door and goes to the cabinet, pulling a coffee cup down. "Oh, come on," he says. "She's just worried about you."

"That gives her some kind of right to make you fly home?"

"She's your best friend, Caggs. She just needed a little reinforcement. Someone to assess the situation." He turns to me, a big grin on his face. I don't mirror it.

"This is so ridiculous. I'm actually happy for the first time in—"

Peter holds up his hands. "Look, no judgment. But Claire's got pretty good instincts."

"You're kidding me. Instincts? The girl doesn't know which way is south without a cab."

Peter pours some coffee into the top of the percolator and flips the cap down. "That's a little harsh."

"Do you know the guys she dates? She thinks she's in love once a week."

Something passes over Peter's face, like the shadow of a cloud. "Do you?" he asks.

"What?"

"Think you're in love."

I play with the drawstring on my pajama bottoms and go take a seat at the counter. I feel like we're little kids again when I say, "None of your business."

Peter whistles. "Who is this Astor guy, anyway?"

"A guy," I say, looking up. "He used to go to school with you, actually."

Peter frowns. "Kensington?"

I shake my head. "Prep."

"Ah." Peter nods. "Last name?"

"He's a senior, not a serial killer, Pete," I say. "He wouldn't have been your year, anyway. I doubt you'd remember."

I'm reminded of the night I met Astor. Of how he remembered not only my brother, but me. It makes me feel better. Like I'm right and Peter is, well, wrong.

Peter pours himself a cup of coffee and holds the canister out to me. "Want some?"

"I'm good, thanks."

Peter sighs and turns around, leaning against the counter. "Don't be pissed. I'm just trying to look out for you."

I raise my eyebrows. "Whose rescue are you running to here, anyway? Mine or Claire's?"

Peter pretends to be shocked by this. "Can't a brother just do something nice for his sis?"

"Buy me a present," I deadpan.

He crosses his arms. He seems to have gotten even bigger since the summer. His T-shirt looks like it's stretching too far. It hits me again. Sometimes it does around Peter. The realization that she won't age. That I'll never know what Hayley looks like as a teenager, as a grown-up. I won't know whether she turns blonde like me, how tall she gets, if she fills out around the middle. She'll never grow up. She'll never be a snarky high schooler, or have a boyfriend, or see the world for what it really is. She'll be ten years old forever.

Peter looks at me, and all the pretense seems to drain out of his eyes, so what's left is what he really means. "I just want to make sure you're okay," he says quietly.

I want to tell him I understand. To put my arms around him and tell him that I love him. That he's all I have left too. But I can't. It's different for Peter. Peter doesn't carry the guilt like I do. He doesn't have to. His grief is pure, plain, simple. It was like the second she died, she became two different people—the sister he lost, and the one I did. Peter didn't see her at the bottom of our pool. He didn't drag her out. He doesn't know what her gray lips looked like. He doesn't know what it feels like to have failed her. How could he understand? How could we share this?

I turn away from him, hop off the stool, and busy myself with getting a water glass out of the cabinet above the sink. "Does Mom know you're home?" I ask.

"Yeah," he says. "We're all having dinner tonight."

I fill the glass and stand with my back to Peter. There is a school dance tonight. Normally I'm not a really big fan of these things, but I convinced Astor to go. It's going to be at the Whitney Museum, in their downstairs event space. I've been looking forward to it because they're keeping the museum open. I'm imagining Astor and me stealing upstairs, getting lost together between Hopper and O'Keefe.

"I can't," I say.

I hear the opening and closing of the pantry door. Peter doesn't say anything. I turn back around. "Sorry," I say. "School dance."

"Since when are you Miss Teen Spirit?" Peter asks.

"It's my last year of high school," I say. "Aren't I allowed to have some of these memories?"

He looks at me, and for a moment I see her eyes. Hayley's. Peter and Hayley always looked way more alike than either of us did. Peter has a lot of my dad. Hayley did too. Rounded features, freckles. And those hazel eyes—always blazing and brilliant. "Of course you are," he says. "Just don't forget your family, eh?"

I don't say what I want to: I wish I could.

CHAPTER ELEVEN

"So are you totally sick of hearing about this?" I ask. I'm on the phone with Astor, relating today's Peter episode. I didn't get to fill him in at school. I'm also rifling through my closet trying to pick out what to wear to the dance tonight. All my clothes feel dull—like they've been run through the washing machine too many times. If I was on better terms with Claire, I'd call her and ask her to bring something over, or she'd have something messengered from Barneys or Bendel's. But we didn't talk today, either, and I don't know what to say to her. I don't really want to say anything.

"Let's run away," Astor says.

"Funny," I say. I pause to examine a black dress my

mother brought me back from a trip to Paris last year. It's a little bit much.

"Come on," he says. "We could go to Rome for the weekend." Astor has been on this kick for a while—going somewhere. Paris. London. Prague. Just the two of us. It's romantic, I'll admit, but I think even *my* parents would notice if I disappeared to another country.

"We can't go to Rome," I say. "We have the school dance tonight."

There is silence on the other end of the line.

"What?" I say.

I hear him inhale. "I don't know if I'm going to be able to make it tonight."

I drop my hand from a green silk dress. "Why?"

"I have some family stuff to deal with." He doesn't offer anything more. Standing in my closet now, I'm surprised at the level of disappointment I feel. I don't know why I care so much. It's just a dance, at a school I don't like, with people I barely know.

"Can I do anything?"

"No," he says. "It's no big deal."

"Oh."

"You're not mad, are you? Do you really want to go to this thing?"

I look at the line of hanging dresses. The discarded heels on the floor. "I don't know."

"It's Kensington," he says. "It's lame. " He drops his voice down. "Why don't I just come over later?"

"Because I wanted to go," I say. The words surprise me, but I don't try to cover them.

I hear Astor breathing on the other end. "I didn't really think you cared," he says. His voice sounds clipped. Maybe even bitter. "You hate this stuff. We both do. It's just a night of having to be fake to people."

I cover. "I get it," I say. "It's fine."

"It's obviously not," he says. He sounds far off, like he's put the phone on speaker. "I'll go."

"You don't have to. You should deal with your family."

He ignores me. "I have to meet you there, though. Okay?"

"Sure," I say. "But if you can't come, that's okay too."

"No, it's not," he says. His voice has changed, softened. "I'll see you soon." He hangs up quickly, before I have a chance to say good-bye.

I feel uneasy. I fight the urge to call him back and tell him I was kidding, I don't really want to go, and why doesn't he just come over after and watch a movie? But I don't. I'd just sound psychotic, I think. Plus I kind of *do* want to go. I want to dance with him. I want him to hold me underneath the lights. I want to feel like maybe this can be something normal. Something real.

I sit down cross-legged on the floor and flip open my

jewelry box. I peer inside. It's a mess, just like I thought—everything jumbled and tangled like the rat's nest my hair sometimes becomes if I've been wearing it down. It's impossible to tell one necklace from another. I hear my mother's voice in my head: *These are nice things, Caggie. You really should take better care of them.*

My mother has always been a collector. She buys the old stuff—antique, art deco. When I was younger she used to take me to the markets in Paris, the Marché aux Puces, and scour the stands for finds. Whenever we'd go on a trip we'd find the jewelry district and spend at least one full afternoon there. The souks in Morocco, the gems district in Bangkok. It was something we did together, just the two of us. She'd always buy me a present, too. Something to remember the trip by.

We haven't done it this year, though. My mother shops a lot at Ralph Lauren now. They started designing stuff that looks like the antiques, so she buys that instead.

I find a pendant necklace entwined with pearls and a chain-link bracelet I got for my sweet sixteen. I pick them apart and hold the pendant in my palm. It's green—an emerald, I think—and about the size of my thumbnail. It's on a silver chain. My dad gave it to me. It was his mother's, but somewhere along the line the original chain got lost. I remember my mom laughing, "It would be like your father to give you a gem with no way to wear it," and taking me to get a new chain. Hayley insisted on coming too.

We went to Tiffany's, which was unusual for my mom—Tiffany's was too mainstream for her—but Hayley wanted to go. She was on an Audrey Hepburn kick. She'd made Trevor and me watch *Breakfast at Tiffany's* about ten times. I told her she could pick where we went; it didn't matter to me. So she picked Tiffany's. She made us get all dolled up before we left too. Black cocktail dresses and gloves and hats. She even borrowed a pair of my mom's big sunglasses. I remember they kept sliding down her nose.

We each chose a silver chain. My mom told Hayley that since she had come with us she could pick out something special. Anything she wanted, within reason. But Hayley chose that silver chain. She wanted the same thing I was getting. My mom tried to explain to her that mine would have a pendant on it, but she didn't care. She wanted to buy what I was buying.

Hayley was independent, definitely, but she was like that with me sometimes. It wasn't that she wanted what I had. She wasn't jealous. The only five-year-old I knew who never threw a tantrum. She wanted us to match. She wanted similarity. She wanted to share things. It was just a plain chain, and I tried to talk her into something else—after all, she didn't have anything to put on it—but she insisted. One just like mine. My mom ended up buying her a charm later—a little ruby—

but she never put it on. She wanted to wear it plain. "Just like the day we bought it," she said.

I slide the green emerald off and squeeze the stone in my hand. It feels cold, like a frozen penny in my palm. Then I put the chain on. I edge up to the slip of glass on the lid of the jewelry box. I can't see my face at this angle, just my neck. I could be Hayley, I think, as I glance at the chain, shimmering on bare skin. Then I bring my hand up to touch it. My fingers give me away. They're long; they always have been. Hayley's were short, tiny, baby hands. Peter would always tease her about it. "Can you even pick up a fork, Hayley?" "Are you sure you can open that door, Hayley?" It was in good fun, she knew that, but I wonder if he thinks about that now. I wonder if he regrets it.

"Knock knock."

I spin around to see my dad standing in my dressing-room doorway. It shocks me so much I practically snap the necklace off.

"Dad," I say. "Hi."

I don't remember the last time I saw him, but it's been weeks, at least. I can't help but notice how much he's aged this year. His hair is nearly all white—gone is the salt-and-pepper my mom used to say made him look like George Clooney. His suit is wrinkled. It looks too big. I know he must have lost weight, because he gets them all made custom.

I stand and go give him a hug. It's stiff. He doesn't wrap his arms all the way around. You know how I keep saying my dad has been on a plane all the time since January, how he hasn't been here because he doesn't know how to deal with what happened? What I mean is: He doesn't know how to deal with me.

My mom didn't blame me, I knew that. She was devastated. She was inconsolable. But she didn't think it was my fault.

My dad couldn't help it. He's right, too. It *was* my fault. I was the one who said she could come. I was the one who was there. I was the one who didn't realize, who wasn't paying attention—how can I blame him? I've basically sent him away.

"You going out?" he asks me. He keeps his hands by his sides. He tucks them into his pockets.

I nod. "School dance," I say.

"With Trevor?"

I shake my head, but I don't explain.

"I'm only in town for the night," he says. "Peter and I are going to Trattoria Dell'Arte."

Trattoria Dell'Arte is this Italian restaurant near Fifty-Seventh Street that my dad always took the three of us to. My mom hated it, but he loved it. Loves it. Sometimes we'd sneak in a meal before Sunday dinner, the four of us. My mom knew what we were up to, but she never confronted us about it, and if she confronted him, we didn't know. I don't think she did. I think she secretly liked that we spent time without her. That we'd want to do that.

"That'll be fun," I say. I think about them sitting at the table by the window. Two chairs instead of four. All of a sudden I just want to get back on the phone with Astor. To tell him that whatever he wants to do tonight is fine with me as long as we can do it together.

My dad clears his throat. "Well, have fun," he says.

I look up at him. He's still so tall, taller even than Peter. "Thanks," I say.

He leaves, his gray suit sagging. It seems to hold the space of all of the things we cannot see, but that are there.

I leave for the Whitney at seven. It only takes me a few minutes to hail a cab and get there. I enter on the first floor. The walkway up to the door is decorated with rose petals. There are just a few left; the rest have landed on the sidewalk or over the railing, clearly disrupted by the wind. Abigail and Constance are sitting at a folding table against the left-hand side of the entrance.

"Caggs!" Abigail coos when she sees me. She has on a red dress that plunges so far down in the front that when she stands, it reveals her belly button.

"Hey, Abbey."

Constance is busy chatting with Bensen Wool, who has just walked in, and she doesn't look up.

Abigail tilts her head to the side. "Are you here alone?" she asks. She runs her finger down the class list and taps my name.

"No," I say. "I'm meeting Astor." I peer down at her check-in sheet. "Is he, um, here yet?"

Abigail shakes her head no. Then she leans across the table, her top dangerously close to spilling out. "It's so funny you're with him. I'd never put you two together."

She giggles, and looks down at Constance, who is all of a sudden paying attention to us.

"Yeah," I say, "well."

Constance cuts me off. "Is Claire coming?"

"Claire doesn't go here anymore."

Abigail shrugs. "We thought you'd still bring her. Once a Kensington girl, always a Kensington girl. Right?"

"You two used to do everything together," Constance adds.

It's the state-the-obvious twins.

"Have a good night," I say, and then turn right and head downstairs.

The bottom floor of the Guggenheim has an outdoor-indoor event space. Some students are milling around outside, and there are high, round tables set up around the perimeter of the inside. They're each covered in a cream-colored tablecloth with a white-rose centerpiece.

I glance down at the black dress I chose. Something I bought in the Hamptons last summer. It's a halter, with silver straps and one cutout circle at the chest. I've been waiting to "fill out" since the seventh grade and it's never happened. This is probably the sexiest thing I own, and on me it might as well be jeans and a T-shirt. If Claire were here she would pull it down in the front. She might have even pinned it down before we left, so that it could show more of my nonexistent cleavage. Claire would step back and survey me. *Not bad,* she'd say. *I really do my best work on you.* Then I'd throw a shoe at her or something, and we'd start hysterically laughing. I realize that sounds like a movie montage of friendship, but the sad part is it's sorta true. Or it was.

I go over to the bar and pick up a cranberry juice in a wine glass. Sometimes they even have champagne at these things "for the chaperones." Our school makes very little effort to pretend the kids at Kensington don't drink. I take a couple of sips, surveying the scene. Gidget and Bartley are a few tables over, talking to Harrington Priesley and Greg Mathews. I think about going over to them and saying hi, but if I remember correctly, I think they have crushes on these boys. Trevor told me that once. Interrupting while they're trying to flirt doesn't feel like the best "make friends" plan.

I just sort of stand off to the side. Ten minutes pass and Astor doesn't show up. You know what's sad? Standing at a party that is being thrown by your high school, by your own grade, and realizing you don't have a single person to talk to.

Twenty minutes pass.

I wave at Gidget. She smiles, but quickly turns back around to Greg.

Thirty minutes pass. Astor still hasn't arrived.

I set my third cranberry juice down. My black dress now feels like I'm trying too hard. To impress who? It's becoming increasingly clear I don't have a date.

And then I see Kristen. She's standing by the bathrooms, toward the other side of the bar. She has on a light purple dress that looks a little like something Hayley used to own. She looks small, innocent. Too young to be here. All at once, my heart starts racing. Because she's looking at me.

I see her at school, of course—in English, in the halls. But we haven't spoken since that day in Mr. Tenner's class. The day she promised me she wouldn't tell.

I take a deep breath and walk over to her. She straightens up and sets her drink down.

"Hi," I say.

"Hey," she says. "Who are you here with?"

I shrug. "Astor was supposed to meet me, but he hasn't shown up."

"It's pretty, huh?" She gestures toward the dance floor.

I nod. "It is."

"I've always really loved the Whitney," she says. "It's the kind of museum you could see being remembered in. Not too flashy, you know?"

"Do you paint?" I ask.

She looks down at her drink. "Sort of. I mean, yes."

"That's cool," I say. "I didn't know."

She raises her shoulders as if to say, *you never asked*.

"So how are you?" I ask.

"Good," she says. She shuffles her feet. I notice she's avoiding making eye contact.

"That doesn't sound awesome," I say.

She shrugs. "It's fine. It's not your problem."

"I think we're a little past that," I say. I realize, suddenly, that she's not going to tell what happened in May, that she never will. The realization strikes me right through the stomach. It makes me grateful and relieved and guilty; all at once.

She laughs. It makes her sound older. A little more solid. "I guess so." She turns to me. "It's not that I ever had too many friends here. But I'm so sick of Abigail and Constance."

"Amen," I say. "I feel you on that one." I raise my glass to hers and we clink.

"Right?" she says. She loosens up a little. Her tone gets higher.

"You just have to ignore them," I say.

She sighs. "I know. It's hard sometimes. The other day I was coming out of the *Journal* and they . . ." She pauses, glances at me.

"Are you working with Trevor?" I ask.

She nips her bottom lip. "Yeah," she says. "They needed a sub. I'm just helping out. I'm sorry, I thought you knew."

"No, no," I say. "That's good. That's great."

She nods a few times. "It's been fun," she says. "Trevor has been telling me some of your ideas. They're really good."

"Thanks," I say. "But most of them were his."

Kristen squints at me, then shakes her head. "That's not what he said."

"He's just being modest," I say. My mouth feels dry. I suddenly want to get out of here.

"He's a really nice guy."

I swallow. "Yeah," I say. "I know."

Then Kristen touches my arm. It startles me to feel her fingertips like this. "We just talk about the *Journal*," she says. "In case you were wondering. He won't even let Mrs. Lancaster assign me to your position. I think he still thinks you're coming back."

I open my mouth to respond, but something stops me.

Trevor is here. He comes in from the outside, laughing with Phil Stern. Our eyes lock instantly, and he smiles. Maybe it's because Astor isn't here, maybe it's because I was standing alone for close to forty minutes, but so do I. I see him relax; I recognize that grin he gets when he's really happy about something. In the next moment Trevor excuses himself from Phil, and then he's making his way over to us.

"Hey," he says. He glances at me and then at Kristen. "How's it going, Jenkins?"

"Pretty good," she says.

Trevor raises his eyebrows at her. "Remember what I told you. If those girls give you lip, you come to me. Yeah?"

She sighs. "I know," she says. "Definitely."

Trevor looks at me. "Hey," he says.

"Hi."

I can hear Kristen clear her throat next to us. "I just remembered I have to relieve the babysitter," she says.

"Oh, come on," Trevor says, knocking her shoulder lightly. "Try a little."

She laughs. It's good to see her smiling. Happy. Alive. "It was nice to see you both." She gives us a half wave and takes off for the stairs. When she's gone, I can feel Trevor close to me.

"You scared her off," I say.

"Nah," he says. "Jenkins is cool. And those rumors about

her are total bullshit." He looks at me, shakes his head in disbelief. "What am I saying? You know that."

"Yeah," I say. "Of course." I suddenly have the intense desire to tell Trevor everything. To spill exactly what happened that night. To tell him how deeply I was hurting—how much I still am. But I know I can't. I'm not even with him anymore. And if he ran away in the spring, this would send him for the moon.

"So how long have you been here?" He's dressed in a gray suit, with a pale pink button-down underneath. I bought him that shirt for Valentine's Day two Februarys ago. We went to Brooks Brothers and picked it out together. I remember I went into the dressing room with him and he pinned me up against the wall. We made out for a while, until some salesman saw us and told us we had to leave. They let us buy the shirt, though, first. "I guess Brooks Brothers is still a business," Trevor joked, stroking my hand.

I wonder if when he puts it on, he thinks about that. I wonder if the link is as direct in his mind as it is in mine.

I shrug. "Not that long, you?"

"An hour or so. I've been outside." He gestures toward the doors, toward where Abigail & Co. are now watching us, whispering.

"Ah," I say. "Cool." I'm not sure I'll ever get used to talking to him like this—like we're just acquaintances. Classmates.

We might as well be commenting about the weather.

"I guess some things haven't changed," he says. He looks up at me. His blue eyes are soft. Familiar.

"Yeah," I say. "I guess not."

We stand there for a moment, just sort of looking at each other. I'm not sure what to say. I don't think he is either. Then the song changes. It's so obvious, really. So predictable that a slow song comes on at this moment, and people start to pair off.

"Do you want to dance?" He's looking at me intently, a small smile on his face.

Astor isn't here. He's probably not even showing. I should have listened to what he was really saying on the phone. He was telling me he didn't want to come tonight. He doesn't want to be here.

"Okay," I say.

Trevor takes my hand. Instantly I get a flashback to our first winter formal. It's like a premonition or something, except from the past. But it's crystal clear—like we're there, right now. The roof of the Gansevoort. The way it felt to have his arms around me, exhilarating and safe all at once. Like being on a ride at an amusement park—even a roller coaster—but knowing you're strapped in. Whatever happens, you're not going anywhere.

Trevor leads me out onto the dance floor and pulls me

close. I let him. I lean my head on his shoulder. He takes my hand in his.

"You look beautiful," he says into my ear.

I want to close my eyes against him. I can feel myself slipping back—back to a time where dancing with Trevor was just what I did, what I should have been doing. When the only thing I had to worry about was where we were going to dinner on Friday night, whose house we were going to study at on Sunday.

With my eyes closed, it almost seems like nothing has changed. I can hear Claire's voice in the background, from a memory: "Hey, lovebirds, Rouge Tomate or Serafina?" The casual way we'd make brunch plans. The ignorant confidence in our forever.

I want to tell him I miss him. I can feel the words bubbling up. Because it's true: I do miss him. I miss this. I miss feeling safe. When I'm in his arms it's like anything could happen—the world could end—and it would somehow be okay.

"Trevor . . . ," I start, and that's when I see Astor.

He's on the landing of the stairs, looking at us. I can see the bewilderment in his eyes, the flash of anger. I don't think; I just tear myself away from Trevor.

"Hey," Trevor says. He doesn't let go of my waist. "What's wrong?"

I'm already trying to move past him, to get to Astor and explain.

"Stop," I say.

Trevor takes a step back, and I can see how hurt he is. It's sharp. It stabs. "Caggie, what—" But then he sees Astor. He reaches out to stop me again, and his fingers land on my arm. "No," he says.

"Let go of me," I say. It comes out harsher than I mean it to. Or maybe exactly like I intend. All I know is that I have to get away from him.

"Caggie, please," he says. "Stay with me."

I look up at him and see the pain in his eyes—the same pain that was there the day he ended things. The day he told me he didn't want to do this anymore.

But Astor is turning to leave, and I don't answer Trevor. I just unlock my arm and race toward Astor, leaving Trevor on the dance floor. I can see other students watching us. I'm sure this is making Abigail's night.

"Astor, wait." I run up the first five steps and grab on to the back of his suit jacket. "We were just dancing," I say.

He spins around. His eyes are dark. They make him look just a little bit scary. "I guess it didn't matter if I came, after all."

"No," I say. I shake my head. "That wasn't what it looked like. Trevor just asked me to dance. We're friends." I'm out of breath. My chest feels shallow, like it's too hard to get air. Lies. Lies. Lies.

"It didn't look too friendly." He continues to climb. I follow behind him until we're in the museum lobby.

"You're wrong," I say. I try not to think about Trevor's words: *Stay with me.* Why? He didn't. "And you weren't even here. You're an hour late, Astor."

This makes him turn around. "I told you I had family stuff," he says. "Who cares about this stupid dance?"

"I do," I say, because it's true. "I care."

He runs a hand over his forehead. I watch him, as he deflates like a tire. "I'm sorry," he says finally. He lifts his eyes up to meet mine. "You look incredible, by the way."

I feel myself exhale. Relief.

"Yeah?"

He tilts his head to the side. "Why do you think I got so mad about Trevor? You're too hot to be in somebody else's arms."

I don't think; I just reach out and pull him down toward me. Talking to Kristen, seeing Trevor—it's all just too much. Too real. Right now I want to disappear. I don't want to think about the past; I want to be here. Astor can help with that. He *does* help with that.

We keep our lips locked. The thing about kissing Astor that I never had with Trevor is this feeling of confidence. Power. I can tell by the way he's looking at me when we break apart—running his eyes over my collarbone, and then up to my lips—that he wants me. And it feels good. Intoxicating. It makes me want to do things I haven't before. It makes me feel like I'm not quite myself. Like I'm slightly different— older, maybe. Not someone who sleeps with a night-light on and still wears a retainer but someone who dates a mystery man from London with a (troubled?) past. It's better than the alternative.

"Let's go," I whisper. I put my lips right up against his ear. "I want to go to your house."

He draws me close to him. He kisses me, runs his hands across my shoulders and down my back. I reach up and wrap my arms around him. He pulls back after a moment, touches his nose to mine.

"Let's," he says.

I realize I'm holding on to him, my hands on his shoulders, my fingers gripping his skin. Even my eyes are tight to him— locked, like they're keeping him in place.

As we make our way to the doors, I glance back at the stairs. I don't know why I do it, because I know what I'll see. Sure enough, Trevor is standing on the top platform, his hands hanging by his sides, staring at us. I don't permit myself his gaze, though, not even for a moment. Instead I grab Astor's hand and lead him out through the museum doors.

"Sixty-Eighth and Lex," Astor tells the cabdriver.

My heart leaps a little, like a kid on a trampoline. That has to be his house. *I'm going to see where he lives.*

He leans his face down and touches his lips to mine. Neither of us says anything.

Four minutes later we pull up at a town house. He hands the cabdriver a ten-dollar bill, and we slide out. "Home sweet," he says. "Come on."

The nerves I felt in the cab seem to be hot-wired once we step outside. Fired up and ready. I'm not sure what I'm expecting inside, but if he's had something to hide, aren't I about to find out what it is? Astor propels me forward.

We climb the stoop steps, and then he punches in a code, 0215, and the door clicks unlocked. February fifteenth. I think it's his birthday.

The foyer is impressive. Bigger than ours by at least ten feet. It's more formal, too. It looks a little like those sitting rooms you see on tours of old palaces—the ones that are staged to look like what might have been during the time period. Bedrooms and living rooms for people who died decades ago. Maybe even centuries.

"This way." He leads me up a wide marble staircase that spills into a long hallway. It looks exactly like a hotel floor. Identical doors marching away in both directions.

"Is anyone home?" I ask. I keep my voice quiet. His house seems like it would carry an echo, and since I've never met his parents, I don't exactly want to run into them in their house at nine o'clock at night heading into their son's room.

"No," he says.

I edge myself closer to him as we move down the hallway. It's not that the house isn't well lit, it is, but it feels dark. Almost haunted.

"In here." He opens one of the matching doors and holds it while I step inside his bedroom.

The contrast is drastic between his room and the rest of the house. While the hallway is bold—all reds and golds and grays—his bedroom is a soft blue. It's also fairly small. Four walls, a closet on one side, and a desk on the other. There is something old about the room—it feels like it's been worn in. The curtains look like they haven't been replaced since he was a baby, and the lampshade is yellowed at the base. I pick up a pad of paper on his dresser and run my hand over the embossed letters. *CWA*.

"So this is it," he says. "You know everything about me now."

I laugh. "This is everything?"

"I already told you about the *Annie* thing, okay?" Astor confided that when he was younger, he used to watch *Annie* on repeat. I've already promised to take him to see it on Broadway. He sits down on his bed, and I hear the springs creak under him. "You're tough to please."

I make my way around the room. I walk gingerly, like

if I step too hard or move my hands too quickly I'll upset the air molecules, and things will appear different than they really are.

I note his bed: pressed white cotton, the expensive kind my mother buys. Probably Pratesi or Frette. His desk: rolltop, light wood. The top is up, and there is a picture inside of him and a woman. I move closer and pick the frame up.

"Come here," he says at the same time as I ask, "Who is this?"

He's quiet behind me, and I turn around, the photo in my hands. It's clearly him, but he's young, maybe four or five years younger than he is now. He's smiling up at the woman, his arms around her middle.

He looks at the photo, then at me.

"Your mother?" I say. I know just by asking that the real question is something else. Maybe I've known all along; I've just been too scared to say it out loud.

He looks up at me and smiles. "Yeah," he says. And then: "Well, it was."

There is a code among people who have lost someone close to them. You don't have to watch your words. If you screw up, if you say the wrong thing, it's okay, because you've lost someone too. You've had someone die on you. You know there are no right answers. Just worse and worse. But you have the right to ask, if you want to. I don't know why, but you do.

I go over to him, sit right down on the edge of the bed and take his hand in mine.

"She died," he says. "Cancer. It was five years ago." I keep still and quiet, like he's a deer I don't want to run. He shakes his head. "It was a long disease; she was sick for a year, even longer." He squeezes my hand. "It's strange, isn't it? I still sometimes expect her to walk through the door."

This is why he hasn't made me talk about Hayley. He knows what it feels like to experience grief, the kind that kills.

"Yes," I say. "It is."

"It changes you," he says. "I mean, I'm not the same person that I was before. Nothing is the same. I tried to explain that to people. To my dad, even—"

All at once, I take his face in my hands. I just put my palms right on his cheeks and search his eyes with mine. "I'm so sorry," I say. Because I am, and I know—all of it. The blame. The guilt. The longing. The distance that death creates between the people who are still here.

He covers my hands with his. "Thank you."

"Is that why you moved to London?"

He nods. "Yeah. We left right after. My dad wanted to stay in New York, but it . . . didn't work." He looks at the floor, then back up at me.

I run my thumb across his cheek. I don't know what to say, and I understand, slowly, that I don't actually have to

THE EDGE OF FALLING

say anything. I understand him. In a way I've never been understood. The reality of this loss, of what it means, is like a string that ties us together. The grief weaving its way from my heart to his.

It's like we're connected by this black core, this ground zero of humanity that's raw and human and strong and fragile all at once. It's life itself—the promise of death, just a heartbeat away, folded into every moment.

"Hey," he says into my ear. He places his hands on either side of my face and brushes my hair back. "Can I tell you something?"

"Please."

He keeps his head down so I can't see his lips, just feel them. "I think I'm in love with you."

I swear, my heart stops. Like a car slamming on the brakes at a red light. "You think?" I manage.

He pulls back. Smiles. "What do you think?"

I told Trevor I loved him immediately. After six days. And then we said it all the time. Constantly. At night on the phone, at school, in the mornings when we saw each other across the park. I meant it too. I did. I loved him. I loved how safe he made me feel, and how well he knew me. I loved that he could anticipate things. Like whether I wanted chocolate ice cream after school or movie tickets to a chick flick I'd never admit I wanted to see.

With Astor it's different. He changes me, or I change him. I'm not sure. All I know is that when I'm with him, I feel like I'm a part of something else. I feel, for the first time since Hayley died, like I'm not alone.

"I think I love you, too," I say.

He runs his hands up my back. "There is a lot of thinking going on here."

I put my hands on his shoulders and let him kiss my neck. "Yeah, what should we do about that?"

He exhales. "What do you want to do about it?"

I know what I want to do. I've known since the first time he walked me home. I want to be close to him, as close as two people can be. Now I know what has happened to him, too. And it's this reality that tugs me closer to him, pulls me down on the blankets with him. Something deep and important and eternal. Something that cannot be taken away.

I feel like I can't breathe, but I don't care. I want him to crush me. To breathe through me, for me. Trevor tried, so did Claire, but they failed because you can't breathe for someone whose needs you don't understand. It's like giving blood type A to an O negative. It doesn't work.

I think, in that moment, lying under him, that Astor could save me. He could save me with the sheer magnitude of what it means to understand. And I'd let him.

195

CHAPTER TWELVE

I wake up in Astor's bed, my dress on the floor, the sheets tangled around me. The clock reads 6:58 a.m., which means if I leave right now I'll still have time to grab my bag at home before school. I roll over. He's sleeping next to me—his face in the pillow, his hand outstretched toward the floor like he's reaching for something.

I crawl out of bed slowly, put on my dress, grab my bag, and edge toward the door. He doesn't move when I open it, and I can still hear him lightly snoring when I'm on the other side.

I sneak down the hallway and into that formal foyer. The only sound in the entire town house is my own breathing, light and short. I'm not sure why I feel like I'm escaping.

I nearly make it to the door when something stops me cold. A man's voice coming from behind the living room door, no more than five feet from me. He's talking loudly, animatedly, like he's not aware he lives in a museum. I was right: This house definitely carries an echo.

"This wasn't supposed to be a permanent solution!" he bellows.

The door is only a few feet away, but I can't seem to make my legs move to get there.

"I told you he needs that. Are there no records in your office?"

My hands feel numb, and when I look down, I see that they've started to shake. They vibrate back and forth, and I clasp them together to stop them from moving. I'm afraid they'll hit something. An expensive lamp. A hidden light switch. I just need to get to the door.

"He isn't stable here," he says. "He needs help. I thought you fucking offered that!"

I hear the phone slam down, and at the same time I bolt for the door. I tear it open and run down the steps and sprint the three and a half blocks home. I don't stop to look whether his father has heard. If he's opened the door. I knock into people on Park Avenue. I whack a woman's handbag off her arm and a little girl starts crying. I mumble an "I'm sorry" over my shoulder.

When I get back, safely locked inside our town house, I'm panting, and my feet, stuffed into last night's heels, are searing pain.

Peter is in the kitchen, a mug of coffee in one hand, a *New Yorker* in the other. Something about the way he's sitting, quiet, unmoving, makes me think that he's waiting for me. Between everything that's happened since I saw him, I completely forgot he was even in town.

"You scared me," I say. My heart is still hammering, and my neck is damp, like I've just woken up from a nightmare. I drop my bag down on the counter next to him and go to pour myself a glass of water. When I turn the tap, my hands are still trembling.

"Where were you?" he asks. He folds the magazine down on the counter. I hear it drop.

His voice sounds rough, gravelly, and I know without looking at him that his eyes are bloodshot. He didn't sleep last night. Maybe he waited up at the counter. I wouldn't put it past him.

"Nowhere," I say, letting the water continue to run. It fills the glass and then begins spilling over. I don't turn it off.

"You didn't come home," he says. "Obviously you were somewhere. "

I take the glass and pour out the top, turning the faucet off. "I was with Astor, okay? What are you, Mom?" I wonder if either Mom or Dad is here. If Dad stayed after dinner last night—I doubt it. He hasn't been known to want to wake up in the same house with me this year.

I hear Peter sigh behind me and the clamor of his cup on the marble. "I don't like him."

I spin around. "You don't have to. And that's so lame, Peter. You don't know him."

"Yes, I do." He pinches the bridge of his nose with his thumb and forefinger.

"You pulled his name up from Prep?" I say. "Come on."

"I remembered," he says. "Astor was his middle name. He used to go by Charles, before they moved to Africa."

"London," I correct.

Peter snorts. "Whatever."

I round on him. "They left because his mom died. Whatever you think you know, you don't know anything."

'They left because he turned into a fucking psychopath."

I take a step back. Peter rubs his forehead and sighs. "I'm sorry, Caggs. I hate to be the one to tell you this, but—"

"Just shut up, okay?" I say. I can't help it; I'm starting to scream. "His mother *died*. She died, Peter. And shockingly, he actually felt it. He understands how *I* feel. You'd know what that was like if you had stopped for two goddamn seconds to mourn Hayley."

Peter slides off the stool and stands. "I don't want to see

you get caught up in this," he says calmly. "He's not a good guy. He's disturbed."

I can't believe what I'm hearing. "You think if people aren't all sunshine and flowers then they're not good, but you know what? Some people actually feel real pain."

"What's that supposed to mean?" Peter takes a step toward me. Instinctively I take one forward too. I'm angry. It's shocking. Startling. But I'm hit with the resentment I feel toward him and have felt since he left in September. I'm angry that he was able to be there this summer. I'm angry I'm the one who has to carry the weight of the memory of her last moment.

"You never even grieved," I say. "You just went out there this summer like nothing ever happened."

"I told you I was packing the house up," Peter says. His voice is low and even, but I can tell it's taking effort to maintain. "Someone had to do it."

"I'm glad you were up to the task."

He exhales sharply. "I'm not going to fight you on this."

"Because you're scared?" I ask. "Because you know I'm right?"

"Because no one is right," he says. "I'm not going to use Hayley as some kind of moral scale. It isn't fair."

"To who?"

"To her."

He shakes his head slowly; then he picks his coffee cup up off the counter and leaves the room.

I run up the stairs into my room and yank off my dress. I pull a scrunched uniform skirt from a drawer and yank a button-down out of a dry-cleaning bag. I knot my hair into a clip and slide some low boots on. I don't catch Peter on the way out, and I walk to school in a daze, cursing him the whole way. He thinks he's so morally superior because, what? *Because he isn't the one that's responsible for her death.*

Then there is Astor.

There are a million things that phone call could have been about, of course. It might not have even been about Astor. But I can't seem to come up with a satisfactory alternative to the fact that his father wants to send him away.

His father doesn't get it, just like mine doesn't. Like Peter doesn't. Like my mother doesn't. I just want to see Astor. He'll explain his dad. He'll tell me it's just another one of his plans, that he wants to move to Prague for business and wants to make sure Astor is taken care of. I can see it now. *He's just been worried since Mom died,* Astor'll say. *He wanted to send me somewhere; he thought they could help with that. He dropped it when I told him I'm happy here. With you.*

Yes, it will all be okay.

But he doesn't show up at school, and by fourth period I'm not as convinced of my own story. I start to panic. The story starts to morph. What if his father got to him? Should I have stayed? Warned him? What if they came today to take him away?

I call his cell phone, but it just rings and rings. No voice mail even.

At lunchtime when Abigail asks me to come sit with them in the library, I tell them no. It's starting to get chilly out, the first gusts of early winter wind, and the button-down isn't exactly doing it. I stand by the gates the entire lunch period, seeing if I can spot him around the corner. Twenty minutes in I decide I'm just going to go back to his house. I can't take it. I don't know what my plan will be once I get there, but I know I need to go. I can't sit around waiting for him to disappear. I need to get there before something happens.

Panic starts to rise in my abdomen and travel up my chest. I'm about to clear the gates when I hear a voice behind me.

"Caggie, hang on."

I spin around to find Trevor. He's wearing his North Face fleece over his uniform; he holds two sandwiches in one hand. I didn't notice it last night, but I see now that his hair is longer. It hangs down a little too far in front. If we were together, I'd have him cut it. I used to do that. Whenever his hair got too long, I'd make an appointment for him at my mother's salon. Sometimes he went to Supercuts, but they always made it too short, and Trevor has the nicest hair—it's soft and silky, like butter. You'd think it could melt when you touch it.

So we'd go to Oscar Blandi, this incredibly ritzy salon on Madison Avenue, and talk in fake British accents all the way there. "Darling, do you think they'll have the proper champagne today? I simply cannot get my hair cut without a good bottle." Then I'd sit next to him in one of those swivel chairs and read trashy magazines until he was done. I wonder if he remembers that when he's shaking his hair out of his eyes. I wonder if he'd go alone.

"I brought you this," he says, extending a sandwich to me.

I look at it in his fingers. Tomato and mozzarella. My favorite. My heart is still racing from Astor, from imagining him on a plane out of here. "Hey, are you okay?" Trevor asks me. He moves closer and puts a hand on my arm. "Caggs?"

"I'm not hungry," I manage.

"What's going on?" His hand is still on my arm and he moves it up to cup my shoulder. His touch is soft, familiar. "Caggie, please talk to me."

I shake my head, unable to say anything at all. *I hate my brother. I slept with Astor. Someone is going to take him away.*

"Hey, hey." Trevor moves his arm around my back, and then he's hugging me. I let him. I even tuck my face into the space between his shoulder and neck. "It's okay," he whispers.

I feel my body relax, like the strings that hold me together have slackened off. A marionette unaccompanied. Like last night, my body remembers. It folds into him. It reminds me I've been missing this.

But then memory flares. All the things that happened between us. All the things that happened last night. This morning. The fact that I still need to get to Astor. Astor—the one who has actually been there for me.

"I'm fine," I mutter, breaking us apart. "Thanks."

"You left pretty quickly last night," he says.

I look at my shoes. I bite my lip.

"Hey," he says. His tone is lighter. "I was thinking of leading today's *Journal* meeting with the interview idea. Get the ball rolling on that. What do you think?"

Going to the *Journal* is the last thing on my mind. "I don't know," I say.

"I thought maybe you'd be back in this week," he counters. "Maybe you changed your mind?" He's talking slowly, like he's weighing his words first. Seeing how heavy they are, what impact they'll make.

"I haven't," I say. "I'm sure Kristen's doing a fine job anyway."

Trevor nods once. "So that's it?" He frowns and I see his lightning scar. Whenever he squints and his forehead smooshes together, he gets a little crinkle down it in the shape of a lightning bolt. I used to call him Harry Potter.

"It'll be better without me," I say. I look past him when

I say it, out toward Fifth. I know without seeing that he's gawking at me, his mouth slightly open, his eyes wide. Even thinking about it makes me annoyed. But when I glance back a moment later, he's calm and still.

"I thought you wanted this," he says.

"I did."

He pauses. Inhales. "The *Journal* was important to you."

I cross my arms. "A lot of things were important to me."

"Come on, Caggs, don't do this. Don't throw all that away because—"

"Because?"

"Because of him," he finishes. "He's not worth you, Caggie. And you know it."

I snort. I feel like laughing. Hysterical, manic bursts. "This has nothing to do with him. If you're jealous, Trevor, maybe you should remind yourself that you're the one who ended things."

He shakes his head. "I'm not jealous."

Something inside me sinks. It makes me even angrier. "Because you don't even care enough to feel that. Got it."

Trevor gapes at me. "How could you say that? Do you have any—" He exhales, stopping himself. "I'm not jealous, because I know he doesn't have you. Not in any way that matters."

"I slept with him," I say. I can see the words settle on

Trevor, sink into him like teeth. "Last night," I continue. "After you asked me to stay with you, I slept with someone else." I cross my arms. I can feel my face heat up.

He swallows, but he keeps his eyes on me. "If you still want to be on the *Journal*, come today," he says. "Otherwise Mrs. Lancaster is going to take it to mean you're off."

He turns and starts walking, back inside Kensington. I don't wait to watch him. I turn too, and race in the other direction. I hail a cab. "Sixty-Eighth and Lex," I tell the driver. Whatever panic was distracted by seeing Trevor has resurfaced. I just have to get to Astor. To make sure he's still here.

I punch in a tip, then swipe my credit card through the machine in the cab and wait as it's approved. Then I bolt outside and up Astor's stoop. When I get to his door, I pause. The code. His town house has a code.

I stop and think. I saw him type it in, remembered, what? His birthday. Not Valentine's Day, but close. I close my eyes and call it up: 0215.

But it's breaking and entering to use it.

I only stop for a few seconds, though. Then my fingers are working on their own. The door clicks unlocked. It's not until I'm pulling it open that I think about the possibility that his dad is here. I hear his voice from this morning rattling around inside my brain. Angry. Screaming. Terror chimes in my chest right along with the panic. Right along with my heart.

The house seems quiet and empty, but I know that can be misleading. I don't stop to find out if I'm right, though. I just zip up the stairs and down the hallway, and then I swing Astor's bedroom door open.

Except it isn't his bedroom. I've chosen wrong—all the doors in the hallway look the same—but once I get inside, I'm not thinking about that. I'm not thinking about anything. Because what I see has pushed every prior thought out of my head.

The room is blue, just like his bedroom, but it's brighter—it has been painted more recently. There are some pillows in the far corner—the big kind you can sit on—and one painting with a spotlight over it on the wall. A piece of modern art, all black lines and red squares.

But none of that is what I actually look at.

Against the near wall there is a bench, no bigger than a wide, low coffee table. On it are rows and rows of pictures. Framed, in all different shapes and sizes. One large image sits in the middle, like Buddha on an altar. It's a photo of Astor's mother. They're all photos of Astor's mother.

Her face. Her body. Her smiling. Her looking at the camera head-on. But what makes it disturbing, what makes me want to drop to my knees right there, is that they are only of her. There are no pictures of Astor. No shots of his mother holding him. No images of Christmas morning, portraits of a smiling baby in her arms. All the photos are cropped to cut others out. They're jagged, ridged. Some even have holes.

And there are candles on the table, in between the photos. Long-stemmed ones with gold bases. Dozens of them. They drip down onto the wooden table, newly lit.

Someone has just been in here.

There is a dresser next to the—what? Shrine?—and I make my way over to it. I already know what I will find, but I tear it open anyway. The faint hint of lavender hits me as I pull out sweaters, tops, jeans—all women's clothing. I start to feel sick. Like I've had too many funnel cakes and gotten on some dizzying amusement park ride.

And then on the floor I see it. The framed photo I picked up in Astor's room last night. The one of him with his mother, his arms around her waist. It's lying faceup, but the frame is shattered; like it was thrown down with force. I see Astor underneath the broken glass—smiling, young, happy.

I look from the candles to the dresser to the broken frame on the floor. It's all a big memorial. Like the flowers people leave along the road at the site of car accidents. But there isn't anything sweet about this. Nothing tender. It's creepy, disturbing in a way that makes me back up against the door. And I know this is Astor's work. I know that he took scissors to every one of these pictures, that he lit these candles. That he keeps her wardrobe in a wooden dresser. That he preserves her memory like a corpse.

The same intensity that compelled me to his house just a few minutes earlier now drives me away. It hollers and screams inside me to get out. Run. Go as far from this room as possible. I turn toward the door, but something makes me spin back around. The photo. I can't leave it on the floor like that. It feels wrong somehow, disrespectful. I bend down and pick it up in my hands, careful to avoid the sharp edges. I layer the stray glass shards on top of the frame, and then I set the whole thing down on the altar. I close my eyes as I leave the room. I don't want to remember what's inside.

CHAPTER THIRTEEN

I call out to Peter when I get home. I want to see him, to tell him what I have found, to tell him I'm sorry. But our house is quiet. As quiet as Astor's. Peter is gone.

I sit down on our stairs, put my elbows on my knees, and take a few deep breaths—inhale and exhale. Anxiety sweeps over me, tugs at my center, and radiates out my limbs. The feeling of slow panic mixed with deep-seated sadness—the kind that makes me want to flee the country at the same time as I want to go upstairs, pull the covers over my head, and never come out. I keep seeing those pieces of shattered glass on the floor. The photos. The sweaters kept like mummies wrapped and pickled in their cases.

My phone lights up—Astor calling. His face pops up on

the screen, his black eyes piercing. It makes my heart beat frantically.

I hit ignore and exhale the breath I've been holding. I have no idea what to do. Am I overreacting? Is it possible this, too, has an explanation?

My phone rings again. Astor. I pick it up with shaky hands and hit the green button this time. My fingers work without me, like they did on the keypad of his town house.

"Caggs?" His voice is sweet on the phone, liquid, like it's pouring through.

I clear my throat. "Hi."

"I just saw all your missed calls," he says. "Is everything okay?"

I hike my shoulder up to keep my cell in place and sit on both my palms, digging my nails into the backs of my legs. "Sure," I say. "Yeah. You didn't come to school."

"I got caught up," he says. Then he lowers his voice. "You ran out so fast this morning I didn't get a chance to tell you."

"What?" I can't even hear my own voice over the beat of my heart.

"I had some appointments today and had to call in." He stops; I hear him breathe. "I'm all done now, though; can I see you?"

"It's the middle of the afternoon."

"But you're not at Kensington."

I yank my hands out from under me and look around, panicked. How does he know? Is he here? Can he see me?

I swallow. "Yes I am."

"No, you're not," he says.

"How do you know that?" I know I'm being ridiculous, but I can't seem to convince my pulse. It lurches forward, like it's prepping me to run.

"Because I'm here." He pauses. "I came to drop off an assignment for fifth period. Is everything okay, Caggs? You're acting kind of strange."

My mind is working overtime trying to convince me of a million opposing things. He understands me. He's dangerous. He's grieving. I don't know which to believe.

"Look, I'm gonna come over," he says. "You home?"

I answer automatically. "Yes."

I'll give him the chance to explain it all to me. Why his dad wants to send him away, and why he has a shrine to his mother. He's my boyfriend; the least he deserves is a chance to tell me what is going on. I'll listen. There are always reasons things are the way they are. I think about Kristen on that rooftop. I think about *me* on that rooftop. About what people believed. People assumed what they saw was real, and they were wrong.

"I'm on my way."

I let my hand go slack and the phone fall. I don't get up. I hug my knees to my chest. I wait.

It took the paramedics five minutes to get to our house the night Hayley drowned. I pulled her out of the pool and called 911 on my cell. I explained to them what had happened, with Hayley in my arms. I gave her CPR. I knew she was dead, but I couldn't bring myself to tell them. I thought if they knew there was no hope it would take them longer to get there.

They were calm when they came in. One of them took me off Hayley and the other put his hands on her. Not on her chest, though, on the sides of her face. They didn't give her CPR. They didn't compress her ribs. One of them asked me what had happened and I told him. He asked me how long it had been and I said I didn't know. Then they asked where my parents were, and if I had called them. How do you tell your parents you lost their child? How do you tell them that you weren't paying attention, you failed, and their daughter has died? How do you tell them you didn't save her? That you were too busy thinking about your boyfriend and your homework and what to make for dinner to notice their ten-year-old girl was drowning?

The police called them. I didn't hear what happened on the other end of the line. I just know that my mother collapsed. They brought her to the hospital, the same one where they took my sister's body.

I'd be lying to you if I said I didn't remember everything from that time—those hours, days. I do. I remember the screams and the hushed voices and the fights. I remember the paramedic who had come to the house talking to one of the police officers. He probably thought he was out of ear-shot when he said, "For the rest of her life, that girl is going to wish she had died instead."

I'm still on the steps when Astor rings the bell ten minutes later. I get up and walk to the door slowly, and pull it open.

He has on corduroys and a light pink oxford shirt with the Polo horse embroidered on the pocket. Brown leather belt. Brown loafers. Slight smile. Slick hair. Same as always.

"Hey." He pulls me toward him and I fold, just a little. It's not the same as last night, though. Something is different, and we can both feel it. Something has slipped into the impossibly small space between us. Or maybe it's the space itself I feel.

I pull back. "Come in."

He tilts his head to the side and purses his eyebrows, but he follows me in. "How was your day?" he asks.

I shrug. "Good."

He takes my hand, swings me around to him. "God, I missed you." He starts kissing me, his hands strong on my back. He presses his lips to my cheek, touches his forehead to mine. "Last night was really great." He takes my hand and sets it up against his chest. I can feel his heart beating—steady and strong.

"I went to your house." The words just fall out. China

cups from an unhinged cabinet shelf. They're loud as they crash.

He pulls back and looks at me, takes my face in his hands. "Hey, what's going on?"

I peel his hands off me and hold them down in front of us. Between us. "I went to your house to see if you were there. I was worried you . . ." My voice trails off. He doesn't know about this morning, about what I heard his father say on the phone.

"Hey, hey." He squeezes my hand. "Whatever you have to tell me, it's okay."

"I saw that room." I drop my gaze to the floor and stare at my feet. They feel like they're getting closer. Like I'm shrinking down toward them.

"What room?" His hands are still in mine, but his voice is cold. Like it's dropped twenty degrees in the last half second.

I look up at him. "The one with the altar to your mother, Astor."

He blinks, drops my arms, but his face doesn't change. "Why were you in there?"

"I was trying to find you."

He shakes his head, just slightly. "That's not really any of your business." He turns away from me and goes to sit on the stairs. He folds his arms across his chest and leans his head back. "Jesus," he says. He says it again.

I stand above him, my feet shuffling side to side. "I know, but I thought it was your bedroom." I pray he doesn't ask how I got into his house to begin with. That I'd have a harder time explaining.

He pinches the bridge of his nose with his thumb and forefinger. Then he pats the step next to him.

I sit down, press my palms together, and tuck them between my knees.

He rubs his hands over his forehead and then turns to face me. He takes a breath in. So do I. "When she died, my dad wanted to get rid of everything. Clothes, pictures, her jewelry. He wanted to sell the house." Astor closes his eyes. Opens them. "I didn't want to be here either, but I didn't think it was right to just throw it all away. He wanted to make it like she had never existed." He searches my eyes. "I know it sounds out there, but I kept thinking maybe she would come back, you know? Maybe she would come back and she would need this stuff." He shakes his head. "I didn't want to believe she was really gone."

I think about my dad's absence. About his unwillingness to look me in the eye, let alone even be here. I think about the paints in Hayley's studio, about her shoes stacked and tucked away at our door. I remember not wanting to throw away her hair clips in the bathroom or her collection of American Girl dolls. I didn't even want to box them up. Wouldn't I have done anything I could to preserve whatever part of her that was left?

I reach across and take his hand, and when I do, I feel his body relax. "I know," I whisper. "I understand. When Hayley died, I wanted to keep everything."

"Did you?" His eyes look bright. Hopeful, even. I understand he's asking me about more than her stuff.

But I can't lie. Not this time. Not with him. "No," I say. "Not like this."

Grief is a strange thing. It torments you. Harasses you incessantly about what you could have done differently. You begin to believe things that you know aren't possible. You believe that you cannot throw away your dead sister's raincoat because she will need it when she comes back. It's almost impossible to think about the finality of death, to wrap your head around forever.

Astor looks up at me, and his eyes are sad. Heartbroken, even. He looks younger than he ever has. Younger than he did that night I met him. Younger than a senior in high school, even. "I know it looks creepy. I'm sorry you saw it. It's just all I have left of her." He exhales, runs his free hand over his lips.

"I used to think there was something I could do to bring her back," I say. I sit up straighter. "I even went to one of those psychics." Astor keeps looking at me, but he doesn't make a sound. "I found her online, and I went down to her office. Well, it was her apartment. Somewhere in Chinatown. She read my palm and drew cards and told me I had suffered great loss." I shake my head. I almost laugh. "But when I asked to talk to Hayley, she said her spirit had moved on." I look up at him. "I think that's crazier than a room full of photos, don't you?"

He takes my hand in his. Kisses my palm. Then he slides over and collects me into his arms. He holds me tightly. A little too tightly. He holds me like I'm the only fixed point in an ocean.

"I'm sorry," I say. I really mean it.

CHAPTER FOURTEEN

Peter comes home again the next Thursday. Astor and I are supposed to rent a movie at my place, but my mom makes me cancel. Astor seems tense on the phone—he has been since we had the conversation about his mother. He was busy this weekend, so we've only seen each other at school, and our interactions have been brief. I want to talk about it, I know he does too, but I can't—not at school.

Our family has dinner Thursday night. And I'm shocked to find Dad in the study, and then, later still, at the dinner table. He even talks to me. He asks about Astor.

"I hear you're seeing someone new" is what he says, a piece of baked potato on his fork.

"Yeah," I say. I don't look at Peter, but I can tell he's

watching me. I haven't asked him why he's barely spent four consecutive days in California since school started. Now that Astor has explained, I'm angry with Peter again for not getting it. For saying Astor is troubled. He lost his mother. He's damaged, not dark.

"I'd like to meet him," he says.

My mother isn't speaking, but I look at her. "Really?" I say. This is the most interest Dad has shown in my life since January. I can't help the spark of hope that begins to bubble up.

My dad nods. "If he's important to you, sure."

Dad glances at Peter then. I wish he didn't. So badly. I wish I could have believed a little bit longer that his intentions were genuine. That he was maybe just trying to get to know me, my life again. But he just wants to see if Peter was right.

I don't say anything. I just eat my baked potato and steak until Mom pushes back her chair. I follow her, leaving my plate. Peter tries to get up after me, but Dad calls him back to the table.

I lock my door. Astor calls, but I don't pick up. I don't want to talk. Not now. When Peter knocks, I don't answer. I pretend to be asleep; it's the best I can come up with.

I know I should, but I don't call Astor back, and I go to school Friday morning with a pit in my stomach the size of a peach. It sits there—leaden, hard.

But lucky for me, Astor isn't at school. I can't help but notice that this time his absence makes me feel calmer, looser. Freer, maybe.

Second period. English.

I'm listening to Mr. Tenner, and it's pretty soothing. He kind of has the perfect voice. I know that's a weird thing to say, and it's not like I have a crush on Mr. Tenner or anything. I once heard Abigail say that he's the most bangable teacher at school, but that was Abigail, not me. There is something about his voice, though. It's deep, but not droning. It's calming, but it doesn't put you to sleep.

Today is the last day of our week on *Mrs. Dalloway*. I didn't read it this time, but I have before because Trevor loves Virginia Woolf. *To the Lighthouse* is his favorite novel. I read it last summer, but I didn't really get it. She's hard to follow. Trevor told me she writes her way into you. "It's like she begins to think through you," he said. "She anticipates what's going on in your head."

I remember we were in the park, spread out on a picnic blanket, my head resting on his stomach. I was holding the book straight above me, trying to block out the sun.

"But we all think differently," I said. "That's impossible."

Trevor leaned down, smiled over me. "It's not, actually," he said. "I believe we're all a lot more alike than you think."

"Please," I said. "The thought processes in my head and in yours are not remotely alike."

"True," Trevor said. "You probably don't constantly think about how gorgeous you are."

"Man," I said. "You are like a bad novel."

Trevor laughed. "It's true, though."

"And what about Claire? She goes from lunch to love in the time it takes me to turn off my alarm."

"Come on," he said. "Just give it a try."

Then he grabbed it out of my hands and started reading to me. His voice isn't like Mr. Tenner's, though, and soon I was fast asleep on his stomach.

I wonder if he remembers. Like with the shirt from Brooks Brothers, I wonder if he's thinking about that right now. He's looking at Mr. Tenner, his lightning scar all lit up on his forehead. I forget I'm staring until he swivels around and looks at me.

I glance sideways at Kristen. She's sitting diagonal to me in the next row, tapping her pen against her notebook. Trevor was wrong. We're not at all alike. We have no idea what other people are thinking, what's going on inside their heads. If we did, someone besides Kristen would have been on Abigail's roof that night.

Tripp and Daniel are bent over something, although I highly doubt it's *Mrs. Dalloway*. I crane closer and see it's the *Post*. They're probably trying to figure out what Jaqueline Delgado was up to last weekend. Whether she's single or not.

Page Six never ceases to provide the hard-hitting news.

Daniel elbows Tripp and they both look up at me. Tripp mouths something, but I can't understand what it is. He's not trying too hard. Then he holds up the tabloid. I squint to look but I can't see. He's pointing to the headline, but it's too far away for me to be able to read.

I shrug and turn my attention back to Mr. Tenner. He's writing some notes on the board and I take them down.

The role of love.

The role of society

Death.

His words morph into memories.

Astor. Hayley. That room full of photos.

I shake my head, trying to clear the frame.

Tripp and Daniel are still whispering, and Constance has gotten in on it. Out of the corner of my eye I see her slide a *Post* out of her bag, nod to them, and slip it back in. What is going on, here? Did some D-list celebrity kick the bucket?

Alexander Hall and Leslie Pewter are also reading it. They glance at me and then at each other. I have the same feeling I had the first day of school when Kristen walked into this classroom. The same one I had the first week back at Kensington in January. Like I'm on exhibit in the Museum of Natural History—stuffed and behind glass.

The chimes go off and people start gathering their stuff.

Constance makes a move to catch up with Tripp, and then glances back at me. She pulls the *Post* out of her bag and hands it to me. "Sorry," she says. Then she's grabbing Daniel's arm, his hand traveling lower down her waist as they disappear into the hall. Trevor glances at me as he swings his backpack over his shoulder, and then Kristen goes over to him. "I had an idea," she says.

He smiles at her and nods. "Mrs. Lancaster said three thirty, by the way. Is that cool?"

"Cool."

They leave side by side, and I stuff the last of my books into my bag.

"Oi, Mcalister." It's Mr. Tenner.

I'm holding the paper in my hands, and I tuck it under my arm, attempting to hide it out of his sight. He raises his eyebrows and waves me over. Great, now I'm going to get in trouble for looking at something that isn't even mine. Thanks a lot, Constance.

"What's up?" I ask. "Great lecture. I'm really enjoying—" But he holds up his hand, cutting me off.

Mr. Tenner takes off his glasses and cleans them on the corner of his shirt. He doesn't tuck his button-downs in. Even among the students at Kensington, that's rare. I think Trevor is one of a lonely few.

"I've always hoped that I'm the kind of teacher who puts

out the 'I'm here for you' vibe." Mr. Tenner says. He peers at me, puts his glasses back on. "Am I right?"

I cross my arms and the newspaper. "Sure," I say. "Yeah, definitely."

"So you know that you could come talk to me, if you needed to."

A few senior girls are lingering by the doors, listening in, and Mr. Tenner gives them a pointed look. They scatter.

He sighs and picks up his briefcase. Underneath is a copy of the *Post*, but it's splayed open, flipped to a middle page. I bend down and look at the headline, and this time I can see it perfectly.

CAULFIELD GRANDDAUGHTER DEEPLY TROUBLED

Mr. Tenner makes a play to grab it, but it's too late. I snatch it up and start reading. They talk about Hayley's death, about the tragedy in the pool, and then my eye skips down a few lines.

Mcalister's friend, reached for comment, told our reporter that Ms. Caulfield has "not been herself since the incident." When asked if she thought Ms. Caulfield was in need of psychological help, the girl sounded simultaneously anxious and resigned. "I think she took Hayley's death badly," the source said. "I don't think she's thinking clearly." Mcalister's friend went on to admit the two girls used to be close but, since Hayley's death, have drifted. "She doesn't want to let anyone in," she said. "It's like she thinks the rest of the world died too." The source, another popular Manhattan socialite, asked to remain anonymous.

I look at Mr. Tenner. He's leaning against the chalkboard, his arms by his sides. "Look," he says, "I don't stake too much on gossip columns, and I know this isn't your first time on the merry-go-round. But it's my personal opinion that all fiction is born of some truth, no matter how small." He peers at me. "Do you get me?"

I can't quite believe the thought forming in my head, but even before it takes shape, I know it's true. I got used to these headlines after Hayley's death. Truthfully, I've been used to them my whole life. But this I have no experience in. Because I've never had a friend sell me out. I don't even think Abigail Adams would go to a reporter. And here, in front of me, printed in the greatest circulating tabloid in Manhattan, is my best friend, Claire Howard, talking trash. I can't think of anything else. The lingering feelings of guilt and terror—

the buzzing from Astor—are replaced with pure, hard-boiled anger.

I want to scream, take up the pages, and hurl them across the room, but instead I turn, calmly, to Mr. Tenner.

"Thank you for your concern," I say through clenched teeth. "But I'm going to be late for physics."

Mr. Tenner nods. "You know, Mcalister, sometimes people do things out of love, even when we can't see it."

I snort. Love. Right. Talking to reporters at the *Post* is really straight from the heart.

"Thanks. Can I go?"

Mr. Tenner nods. "Of course." He takes up his briefcase. "Enjoy physics."

I follow him out of the room and then bolt in the opposite direction. I'm not going to physics. I'm going to find Claire, and then I'm going to make it very clear that if our friendship wasn't over before, if her blatant dislike of Astor and her ratting me out to Peter weren't enough to end it, talking to a tabloid definitely is.

"Watch it!" I whip around to see Abigail holding her hands up like her nails are wet. "Where are you going?" she demands.

I inhale sharply. "Downtown."

Abigail eyes me, then straightens up. "For the record, I always thought Claire was a little gossipy."

I look at Abigail and say something I never, not in a million years, thought I would ever say. "Well, Abbey, it looks like you were right."

She seems surprised, but satisfied, as I duck out the gates.

I get a cab quickly. There isn't too much traffic—it's only late morning, after all—and before I have time to form what, exactly, I'm going to say to Claire, we're at her building.

In the lobby I greet Jeff Bridges, who lets me up. Claire is rarely at school on Fridays. She thinks we should have Fridays off, and she implements a three-day weekend by simply taking one. This happens every week. She should have been kicked out of both Kensington and her downtown school, but every time she gets close, her dad donates some print of Angelina Jolie riding a camel or whatever, it sells for thousands of dollars at the auction, and voila! Claire gets another six months.

"Claire!" I yell when the elevator doors deliver me into her living room.

No answer, which doesn't necessarily mean anything. There is always the roof. Even when it's cold, Claire still hangs out up there.

I rummage the key out of the kitchen drawer and climb the stairs. The door locks from the inside, so if you're upstairs you can be sure no one will come up to disturb you, unless they have the key. Claire says her parents installed that feature to make sure she wouldn't sneak up there herself when she was a little kid.

At the top of the stairs I turn the key and pop the door open.

There is this little alcove by the bar with two stools, where if you spin 180 degrees around you can get a great view of the Empire State Building. I round the corner and then stop dead in my tracks. There is someone up there, all right, but it's not Claire.

"Peter?"

My brother is slumped over a mug, looking out over the river, his feet resting on a stool and a book on his lap.

He leaps up when he sees me, the coffee cup spilling over, the book splaying out on the floor. "What are you doing here?" he asks.

"What are *you* doing here?" I snap back. He's supposed to be at school, in California. Not on gossip-queen Claire's rooftop.

I wait, but no answer.

"I thought you were going back to California today?" I say.

He drops his gaze. "No."

"No, you're not going back today?" I start to raise my voice. I'm already revved up; it's not hard to start. "Peter, what the hell is going on?"

He's got on his old, brown cashmere sweater, the one with the elbow pads. "Peter?" I ask again.

"I'm staying here," he says. He lifts the book off the floor, closes it, and sets it on a chair.

"Staying here?" I walk closer. "What are you talking about?"

He runs a hand over his chin. "I didn't go back to school."

"But . . ." I don't understand. Sure, he's been back more often this semester. Too often. But . . . I open my mouth to verbalize my running mental commentary, but something stops me. Claire's shirt the night we went to Eataly. It wasn't the same kind my brother has. It *was* my brother's.

"How long has this been going on?" I ask.

He blows some air out through his lips. "Which part?"

I feel like laughing. It's all so ridiculous. Peter and Claire. The *Post*. The fact that we've all ended up here. "You choose," I say, my voice dry. "How long have you been back in New York? How long have you been lying to Mom and Dad? How long have you been sleeping with Claire?" I fold my arms across my chest. "Any order."

He inhales, runs his hands over his face. "I didn't enroll for this year," he says. "After the summer I . . ." He clears his throat. "After the summer I went back to LA and I stayed at Jeffrey's."

Malibu. Our uncle. "Why didn't you tell me?" I ask. "You could have come home."

Peter looks at me, and I can read it all. It's like a scary movie I've seen before. I just want to plug my ears at the bad parts. Instead I focus on what I can: "Claire," I say.

"It's not like that," he says. "That's what I've been trying to tell you."

"Oh yeah? What's it like?" My throat feels dry. I have to keep swallowing. "You just decided to shack up with her instead of going to college? You figured, what? Why date Felicia when you can have a high school model? Did you see the *Post*? Do you have any idea what she did to me? To *us*?"

Peter opens his mouth, but I'm on a roll. "And you didn't fly in because you were concerned about me. You just came uptown because Claire opened her big mouth. Convenient."

"Caggs—"

"You deserve each other," I say. "I hope you know you're just the flavor of the month, too. She'll get bored; she always does."

I turn because all of a sudden a new emotion is taking over—the anger giving way, like icicles melting. I can feel the water coming, salty, tangy, and I don't want to be around Peter when it does.

He makes a move to follow me again. "Don't!" I yell over my shoulder.

I don't turn around, but I hear him stop. Silence behind me. Peter is still my brother. He knows when to push it, and when not to. He won't follow me. Not now, anyway.

I run down the stairs and out into the waiting elevator. I don't stop to think where Claire is. I want to get far away from this whole thing. I don't know anyone anymore. Claire's betrayed me. Peter has dropped out of school to be, what? Her professional boyfriend? I can't even think about what my parents would do if they ever found out.

I feel the tears well up again, threatening to spill, but I blink them back and focus on the questions. No matter how much Peter wanted Claire, why would he leave USC? She's in LA all the time. It's completely unlike Peter to drop out of school. He's always been that guy, like Trevor. President of everything, a million extracurricular activities. He wants to be a doctor. I don't think doctors take a leave of absence from college. Not sophomore year, anyway. Without even thinking, I've fallen into the walking game.

Near Fourteenth Street I pass a Starbucks that used to be a specialty grocery store. I used to like that about New York—how quickly things could change. But that was before Hayley. After she died, the city's ability to move on seemed intentional somehow, vengeful.

When I think about last May, about being on that roof, that's the single thing I remember most. The way life seemed to be moving past me, rushing forward. Like a log down a river toward the falls. But I was a rock. Stuck. Everything racing around me, over and under. I couldn't move. I couldn't do anything but hear the rapids—far-off, close, unreachable. It was all the same thing. The future I wouldn't be a part of.

People think those sorts of things are choices. Decisions. Whether you stay stuck or move forward. But they're not. That's the thing about May: It wasn't a choice. It was the absence of choice. Standing up there on that roof I'd never felt so powerless. Hauling Kristen up and over that railing—that was no feat of will. That was a reaction, plain and simple. It wasn't me; it was some old human system, some trick of the brain: autopilot, adrenaline, whatever you want to call it. It's funny how when big things happen, people want to know lots of details. They always have a million questions—what it felt like, how you did it, what you thought about in that moment, hovering a millimeter from death. But they never ask the right ones. Never the ones they should.

No one ever asked me why I went up to Abigail's roof to begin with. Not the *Post*. Not Claire. Not even Abigail herself.

The one question they should have asked they didn't, just like the one question I should have asked that night in January I didn't.

Hayley, where are you?

I keep on walking.

I'm on Seventh Avenue, headed straight for Columbus Circle, when I spot Trevor. He takes violin lessons down in the Fifties, he has forever, and I see him standing on the side-walk, running his foot along the pavement.

It's unfortunate that he is standing here right now. That it had to be him, in this moment. I know what I'm about to do is no good. That I should just keep walking. But I can't stop myself. I don't know how. That's the thing about anger—it's a transformative force. It can bring you back and then get behind you, push you forward. I'm angry with Claire about that article, angry with Peter for lying, but when I see Trevor, holding his music case, his eyes slightly squinting into the sun, all that rage gets directed like water through a funnel—one clear, straight line. His disappointment about the *Journal*, his comments about Astor, his eyes at the dance, standing on the stairs. It all makes me rage. The fact that he's still here. That he reminds me so much about everything I don't have anymore.

I move up to him fast. He's surprised to see me, and he kind of warbles, takes a step back. I've spent months running from him, but now the serendipity of him being on the street feels like destiny finally handing me a card. It's my turn to confront him now. To make him listen to what I have to say.

"Did you read that Page Six piece?" I ask.

"What are you—?" He's still trying to catch up—did I seek him out? Do I remember his violin schedule? Yes, actually, but I don't tell him that.

"Peter is living at Claire's," I continue.

Trevor squints at me but doesn't seem surprised.

"Did you know that?"

He blows some air out through his lips and nods.

"You're kidding me."

"Claire didn't—"

"Who does Claire think she is?" I interrupt. "She's butted into everything. She's run her big mouth all over Manhattan. I thought she was my friend."

Trevor looks at me, incredulous. "You're kidding me."

"Trevor—"

"No. Caggie, I'm sorry, but you have to get this." He steps closer to me, and I see the side of his mouth twitch, the little corner of his cheek flaring the way it does when he's really concerned. I used to watch that cheek when we were studying, saw it wink at me when he first leaned down, close, and told me he loved me. "You don't get it. Claire is the only one who's actually been brave enough to say something. To *do* something. Do you know why Peter is there?"

"No," I admit.

"He didn't want to leave you." Trevor's hair falls into his face, but I can see his eyes staring at me. The purest blue. "He wanted to stay to make sure you were okay."

"That's ridiculous," I say, glancing away. "Why would he do that?"

Trevor exhales. "Come on, Caggie. You're not the only person who lost someone in all of this." He holds his gaze to mine, and I recognize something in it, something I haven't seen in a long time. The way he used to look at me. How I knew how much he cared.

"I know," I say.

He shakes his head. "You don't."

"Of course I do. You're not my brother, Trevor. You're not in this family."

"No, you're right, I'm not. But I was . . ." His voice catches. "I screwed up, Caggie." He steps closer, like he's testing the waters. I don't move. "I should never have left this summer. I should have stayed with you, even if you wouldn't let me in. I should have seen you every day. I should have been *with* you."

I shake my head. I can't deal with this. There is too much spinning. Claire and Peter and Astor, spokes on a wheel turning faster and faster, about to puncture something.

"Look at me," he says.

I pick my head up, just slightly. "Don't do this, Trevor," I say. But it's quiet. Shaky. I'm losing ground.

"I made a mistake," he says. "I thought things would be better for you if I wasn't here."

"How?" I whisper.

"I don't know," he says. He shakes his head. "It was stupid. But you kept pushing me away."

"Trevor . . ."

He looks at me, head-on. "I didn't go to California this summer," he says. "I helped Peter at the beach house."

I gape at him. "What are you talking about?"

"There was no one else to do it. I thought at least that was a way I could help." He steps closer to me still and puts his hand on my elbow. Cups it the way he's done so many times before. "I love you, Caggie. Don't you know that?"

"I . . ."

But in the next instant he kisses me. He puts his hand on the side of my face and one around my waist and draws me close to him. His lips feel like relief. Everything else melts away, and for a moment I'm just focused on what it feels like to be with him. Wonderful, exhilarating. The purest kind of perfect.

But so many things are wrong. We can't just kiss here like nothing happened. We can't just pretend that we can move on to okay when there is so much standing in the way.

"I have to go," I say, pulling back.

Trevor loosens his arms around me. "Caggie, please, can't we talk about this?"

I look at him. Maybe I'm crying. I can't even feel my face. "No," I say. "It's over, Trevor."

He doesn't fight me as I walk away.

I don't know what to think of any of this, so I don't. I

shut my brain off. I turn down Fifty-Eighth Street toward Broadway and then up to Fifty-Ninth. Around the Plaza. We had Hayley's eighth birthday there, in the Eloise Suite. We brought her friends downstairs for high tea. She may have been an artist—sensitive, wise beyond her years—but she was also just a little girl. She loved dressing up in pink, eating sugar cookies, and sliding on white elbow gloves. I remember I put together the gift bags for that birthday: little Eloise totes with her guests' names stenciled on the front. Fake pet turtles, a box of wax crayons, and black patent-leather Mary Janes in each of their sizes.

The next day, when we were checking out, Hayley wanted to know where my gift bag was. I told her the bags were just for her friends. She looked at me, really puzzled, and then said, "But you're my sister."

You're my sister.

Here is the truth. What I can't say to Peter or Trevor or Claire: It doesn't get better; it gets worse. I miss her more every single day. They say absence makes the heart grow fonder, but what about death? What happens when you know there will never come a time when the ache will be alleviated? How do you deal with missing someone forever?

I walk the last eight blocks home, and when I get there, Astor is standing outside. In the chaos of Peter and Claire and Trevor I almost forgot about everything that is going on with him. And that I've avoided about ten of his phone calls. He looks nervous. He's tapping his foot against the pavement like he's trying to chip it away. His shirt is untucked, and his cheeks are flushed. Beads of sweat hang from his forehead.

"Caggie," he says. He sounds like he's been waiting forever.

He pulls me to him as soon as he sees me. Puts his hands around my waist and drags me in like a tow truck. I feel numb. Blank. So overloaded with everything that there isn't space for anything. Even when he starts kissing me—fast, furious—I can barely feel his lips at all.

I try to pull back, but he keeps me close, his arms locked around me. I start to feel like I'm suffocating. He's crushing me, and the more I try to squirm, the tighter he holds me. I suddenly remember something I came across in my Google searches on drowning. How if you're trying to rescue someone from the water, they will try to climb on top of you in order to save themselves. They'll hold you down. Often the people who try to rescue are the ones who end up drowning.

"Stop." I yank myself back far enough to look at him, and the moment our eyes lock, he releases me.

He's still got ahold of my hand, and I let him trace my fingers with his thumb. He glances down the street, then pulls me up onto my front steps. "He found out," he says. His eyes dart back and forth, like someone is watching us.

"I tried to call you. I called you a million times."

"Who?" I ask, groping for time, but I already know he's talking about his dad. The image of the glass frame pops into my mind like red paint lobbed at a white canvas. Loud. Screaming. Sudden. Hysterical, even.

"He found out about what?" I swallow.

"We had a deal," he says.

I get the distinct impression he isn't speaking to me, not really. He's talking to himself, relating the story out loud so it becomes something he can sort through. Pieces of a puzzle he's got to take out of the box and set faceup on the floor.

"My dad and I. If I stayed in school and didn't flunk out this time, I could stay." He glances at me, like it's a look he's stealing. Something that doesn't belong to him. "I thought it would be easier to get my records. I didn't think it would matter, but they kicked me out. Kensington." I hear him swear under his breath.

My stomach bottoms out. I feel sick. It's the same feeling I got standing in his mother's shrine room. I think about his father on the phone. The intensity in his voice. He wanted to send him away. And now, standing here, I know where he wants him to go. I remember Peter's warning: *They left because he turned into a fucking psychopath.*

"I need somewhere to go," he says.

He's still holding tight to my hand, so tight that I'm afraid to look down. I'm afraid his knuckles will be white. That I'll be able to see blood draining.

"Okay," I say. "It's going to be okay." I try to keep my voice level, but it won't stop shaking.

I hate this thought for creeping in. I hate it like I hated every single person who told me after Hayley died that they "were there." I resent it, but that doesn't stop it from coming: Maybe Astor's father is right. Maybe he needs help.

"I need to disappear," he says.

"London?"

He looks at me like he can't believe what I just suggested. "To who?"

"Friends?" I mumble. I'm losing ground. Standing on quicksand. I can tell he has something else in mind, something that is absolutely, unquestionably, not an option.

"I don't want to leave you," he says.

"I don't want you to either," I say. They're just words. I don't even know if they're true.

He pulls me close again. "What do you want to do?" I whisper. I just want him to ask already. Get it out in the open. I know it's coming.

He says it so quietly, so gently, that the words don't make an impact at first. They slip in on silk.

"Your beach house."

It's like all the air gets sucked off the street. I can even hear it whoosh away.

I don't respond, just swallow.

"No one is there," he says. "It's empty; they'd never even know."

I shake my head. "I'm not going out there." That place is a tomb. It's a grave site. It isn't a house; it's the scene of a crime. In my head, when I think about it, I think maybe it doesn't exist anymore. Maybe it died with her. The only time I've talked about the house with him is when I've been complaining about Peter. The fact that he's stored the information makes my chest feel tight.

"Caggie, please. If we don't leave, he's going to send me away." His eyes are fired up, raw. It's like he's come apart at the seams—even his clothing, normally pressed, even, buttoned, has come undone.

I try to move around him, toward the door. The air hasn't returned to the street, and I have the stupid, pathetically hopeful thought that maybe there is air inside. Maybe I'll be able to breathe if I just shut the door.

"Just get on a flight somewhere," I say, fumbling with my keys. "Where does he want you to go, anyway?" But I know. Of course I know. The same place where everyone thought Kristen was this summer. Somewhere they send people who need help.

He grabs my shoulders and spins me around. "He'll track my credit card. I just have to disappear. Just until we can figure out what to do next."

"Are you asking me to run away with you?" But it isn't like when he asked me to go to Paris, or Rome. This isn't romantic. This is desperate.

"Come on, Caggie. What is here for you, anyway?"

My keys are rattling in my hands. Shaking against each other. And when I open my mouth, my words do the same. "I can't go there, Astor."

"You can," he says. He takes my hand in his. Covers it. "I'll be with you. We'll do it together."

"No," I say. I shake my head; my shoulders are quaking. I feel like one of those bobblehead dolls that bounce around on people's desks. "I can't."

He keeps his eyes on me but wraps our fingers together. Threads his through mine. "Please," he says.

I can feel him looking at me, but I keep my gaze down, on our interlaced hands, the keys between us. I can see them wink in the sun, like a penny on the sidewalk. Like the glint of a bracelet at the bottom of a pool. I already know, even before I answer, that I won't use them.

I won't be going back inside.

Because I understand desperation. There is no reasoning with it. It doesn't respond to rationalizations. I could stand on my steps and give him every possible excuse and new plan. I could buy him a plane ticket to India myself. But it won't matter. He's made up his mind. The only place he's going to feel safe is the beach house. Have I mentioned yet? Grief makes you crazy.

"How do you want to go?" I ask. My voice sounds small, resigned. Like it belongs to someone else.

"I'll drive," he says. "I have a car here."

I know that I'm headed straight for disaster. But I do it anyway. I don't know what the alternative is. Just like on that roof, there isn't a choice here. It's forward. And forward is east. The thing about loss, huge grief, is that it can make you feel so blank you become untouchable. It can make you feel like you have nothing left to lose.

CHAPTER FIFTEEN

Astor is driving too fast. It's getting dark on the highway, and although I know the roads well, I also know the Hamptons are a dangerous place to be reckless on the road. A whole bunch of weekend drivers, people who aren't used to being in cars. Dinner parties, alcohol. It's a perfect storm for collisions, and they happen all the time.

"Slow down," I say for what feels like the hundredth time. My words get swallowed up by air. All the windows are down.

Astor seems in a trance. He has for the past hour. Nervous, focused. He barely talks except to occasionally ask me if we're on the right road, if there's a shortcut I know about. If we turn left here, will we still get there?

I have my elbow set in the crease of the open window, my head resting in my hand. I'm keeping my eyes on the road, trying to avoid the memories that come like hot pokers to the skin.

The last time I drove here, Hayley was next to me in the passenger seat. It was about the same time, dusk, but it was probably a bit earlier given how soon the sun sets in January. The roads had been icy—there had been a snowstorm the weekend before—but the day we drove out, January third, was sunny and all the snow melted. I remember because Claire wanted to sit on her roof and see if we could catch a tan.

"It's still going to be like thirty degrees," I said.

"The sun doesn't care whether it's cold or not—it still shines."

The sun does still shine. It did that day and the day after, too. I remember waking up in a hospital and seeing it through the windows, pouring in through the translucent curtains.

People think tragedies are blurs, that they fade together like a film dissolve, but that's not at all how it goes. The memories are sharp, jagged. When you call them up, they could slice right through you.

Hayley was chatty in the car. Too chatty. She wanted to talk about things I didn't, like where I wanted to go to college. I didn't know. The University of Iowa, or somewhere in California, I thought. Close to our uncle. The beach. Somewhere "out west." It's funny to remember that moment before, to think I was trying to escape something even then.

That running from everything didn't begin with her death.

Hayley was also curious about Trevor. She always was. She wanted to talk about him all the time. I remember she was disappointed he wasn't coming out until Saturday morning. I think she had a crush on him. Whatever that means for a ten-year-old. She looked up to him. He would bring her books, talk to her about her painting. Sometimes I think he came over just to see her, and Hayley loved it.

She was smart—far beyond her years. She could hold her own in any discussion: politics, literature, whatever. My parents always wanted to test her IQ—my mom thought she should skip a grade—but Hayley would never let them do it. I think her secret fear was being different from people, separate. She wanted to be involved in everything, even if it didn't concern her. She was independent, but she wanted us around. She wanted company.

I wince as the memory comes back—sharp and cold and as biting as a fresh icicle straight through the heart. I see myself pulling her out of the pool. I see her gray lips. I watch myself hold her in my arms. In her moment of death she was alone. I wasn't there to keep her company. To tell her that it was all going to be okay. That's the thing I regret most. That she died alone.

My phone rings and it shocks me upright. My hand hits the window edge and I yank it back, rubbing it down on my leg.

"Who's that?" Astor wants to know.

He glances at me, his hands tight on the steering wheel.

I reach down and pull open my bag. On the screen I see Trevor's name flashing. I want to pick it up so badly. My finger itches to hit the green button, but I know I can't. Not now. I should have listened when he told me all of that on the sidewalk. I should have let him hold me. Make me stay.

"No one," I lie.

"Obviously someone is calling, Caggie." There is an edge to his tone, a second layer that makes my insides feel cold. It's so stupid that I've never thought of this before. That it's only come to me in the front seat of his car, speeding toward Hayley's grave, but here it is: I don't trust him.

I know what it's like to be where he is. Right on the edge. Anything is possible when you think nothing is left anymore.

"It was just Abigail," I say, hoping my quick breath doesn't give me away. "We're partners for a history project."

He places his free hand on my shoulder. He exhales like he's been holding his breath for hours. "Sorry," he says.

I feel his hand on my arm like the wind. It makes my hairs stand on end, my goose bumps rise up like speed bumps.

I smile back. "We're almost there," I say.

He turns up the music, something low and melodic. I keep my cell phone in my hand. I want to call Claire, Trevor, Peter. I want to hear their voices, to tell them where I am. But

I can't. Not with Astor. He's not stable, and now I know he never was. It didn't start on the sidewalk a few hours ago. It didn't even start with that room in his house. It has just floated up to the surface tonight after being buried for months.

Here's the other thing about grief: It will stay as long as you let it. And if you find someone who wants to hold on too, it will bind you to them. It's fitting, really, how desperately grief does not want to die.

"No one can know where we are," Astor keeps saying.

He swings left and I gesture up ahead. The road splits, and our driveway is down the right-hand side. The ocean side.

I've imagined coming here so many times since January. What it would feel like to turn down this familiar road. To see the headlights sweep left and then settle on our house: gray shingles, white beams, wraparound porch. You can't see the pool from the driveway. It's out back—an infinity pool that seems to run straight into the sea.

"Not too shabby," Astor says.

The house will be boarded up, but I took our spare key. The one Peter and I have kept hidden underneath the flower pot on our front stoop. Peter had it made so we could come out here without our parents knowing. Weekend parties, overnights when I would sneak Trevor up and Claire would cover for me, saying I was sleeping at her place downtown. I was surprised to find it there, although I don't know why. It's not like either one of us has had to use it recently. Not until today, anyway.

Astor kills the lights in the driveway and leans across the seat to me. I can feel the cell phone in my palm, and I squeeze it. Willing it to transport me somewhere far away from here.

He hovers over me. "Hey," he whispers.

What was once sexy, heady, now feels claustrophobic. This car is too small for both of us.

He places a hand on my cheek. Moves farther in to kiss me.

"We made it," I say, because I have to say something.

My voice shakes.

He notices.

"Are you okay, Caggs?" His lips are at my ear.

A flare of anger ignites inside me like a firecracker. Anger at him for using my nickname. Anger at myself for thinking he knew me. For letting him in and ending up back here.

"Let's just go," I say.

He kisses my cheek, then opens the door. I wait for him to come around, and in the time he does, I hold the number 2 key down on my phone. It's Claire's speed dial. I turn the volume down low and pray she picks up. Pray she listens.

Then I slide the phone into my skirt pocket, speaker facing up, and get out of the car.

There is a stone pathway to the front door that usually lights up as soon as you step out of the car (it's set to sensors),

REBECCA SERLE

250

but tonight it doesn't. "The electricity must be off," I mutter.

Astor takes his lighter out of his pocket and flicks it, a lick of flame igniting his features. "Got any candles?" he asks.

I slip the key out of the opposite pocket, the one without the phone, and feel my way to the front door. I slide it in. It gives easily.

The moon off the water illuminates the house, and I see that it's been emptied. There is a sunken living room that used to have two facing couches with a glass coffee table in the middle. The coffee table had floating shells framed in it, something Peter and I had made for Mom on her birthday a few years ago. All the shells we found on our beach—the Hamptons doesn't have too many, so there were big pieces of beach glass in there, too. I remember the coffee table books, one about French cooking and another about interior design, all with uncracked spines. There were shelves on the walls with family pictures and a mantel with two candelabras, purchased on my mother's trip to Belgium.

Now there is nothing here. Not even the light smell of lilac and lavender and garlic that always seemed to linger, even if we hadn't cooked in the house in weeks.

Astor comes up behind me and slips his hands around my waist. "Give me a tour," he murmurs into my ear.

"There isn't much to show anymore," I say. I'm sure with his arms around my chest like this, tight, pulled, that he can feel my heart beating. It's pounding, erratic, like it's attempting to claw its way out of my body, scramble along the floor, and escape out to the dunes.

"What used to be here?" he asks.

I loop his arm over my head, out from me, and step down into the living room. "The kitchen is that way." I gesture right, toward the French doors. We both look down at the empty room, the wood island stranded in the middle of the tile floor like a shipwrecked man.

My eyes are adjusting to the darkness, and when I look at Astor now I can see his features. I never noticed how sharp they were. Chiseled. Like he's been cut from marble.

"Where was Hayley's room?" he asks.

I knew he was going to ask. Astor isn't interested in the family room. He doesn't want to know where we used to keep the board games. But the words still feel like fingers crawling up my spine.

"This way." I swallow.

I lead him away from the kitchen and through the sunken living room, the hallway that used to be lined with family photographs—ones of us swimming in our summers here. I see them like negatives on the walls: Hayley with her giant heart sunglasses on, slipping down her nose. Hayley wearing her water wings, nowhere near the pool.

We round the corner, and then we're in her room. It's empty, of course. No more rocking chair. No easel. No line of clogs or toy chest or coat rack where she used to hang her rain slicker, the yellow one with the polka dots that looked like little stars. It's still carpeted, though, and her drapes are still hanging—big, pink, and billowy. Our mom picked them out. Hayley hated them.

Astor and I stand in the doorway, and when he takes my hand, it startles me. I feel like a ghost here. Like Hayley: untouchable in my translucence.

"Where did they take her things?" he asks me.

"I don't know." I have no idea what Peter did with everything. Where they shipped it. Whether they threw it away or sold it. I think about those clogs and that slicker. The thought of someone else wearing them, or worse, them lying at the bottom of a land-fill, makes my insides feel like they're being wrung out.

Astor tugs me by the arm to the center of the room. He paces around, peers out the window. I'm watching him, trying to read him—any sign of what he might do. Then he goes over to the closet and opens it. "Hey, Caggie," he says. "Looks like they missed something."

I walk toward him slowly. My feet feel like they're made of lead. I hate this. I hate that we are here. He picks up a box. The standard shipping size—two by two by two.

Astor sits down on the floor, pulling me down next to him. He flicks his lighter again, but it doesn't illuminate that much more—my eyes are almost entirely accustomed to the darkness now.

He runs his forefinger along the seam. Wiggles the tape loose.

"Stop," I say, but he doesn't listen.

I can hear the waves crashing. They sound closer than I remember.

He pulls back the top, and then we're both peering inside. It's filled with what looks like trash: Q-tips and a rubber duck and nail-polish remover. I pick up the rubber duck, turn it over. I don't remember Hayley having this. These must be things Peter didn't feel were worth storing.

I'm relieved. It could have been photos. It could have been clothes. The box could have opened and smelled like her.

But then I see a black Mary Jane poking out from the bottom. One of the shoes we bought for her Eloise birthday party. I fish it up. I cup it in my hands. I cradle it there, like an antique—something fragile and expensive.

Astor sets the box down. "How does it feel?" he asks me.

"What?"

"Being here."

I force myself to look at him. "Like I miss her," I say. *Like hell,* I want to add.

"Are you sorry we came?" He runs his eyes over my face. I feel like they leave track marks.

I gawk at him. "You didn't give me any choice."

He leans over to touch me, but I slide back. I think his fingers will be cold. All at once, I don't want them near me.

"Caggie," he says. "It's okay. I understand."

I just keep staring at him. It's like I've never seen him before.

Something is starting to form, bloom in my stomach and climb up to my heart. Astor hasn't asked me to talk about Hayley, he hasn't wanted to know how I'm doing with her death, with what happened in May, but what he's required has been worse. He's offered his loss up like a diamond. He's given it to me, the way Peter gave me his watchful eye, the way Claire gave me her concern. But simply understanding doesn't make it better. Darkness stacked on darkness just makes it that much harder to find the light.

I don't want to live in this place. I don't want my life to be an addendum to her death.

Astor is edging closer to me, and I know, all at once, that there is a good chance I won't make it out of here. That we either won't leave here alive or we won't go back. There are some things from which we don't recover—some places that, once visited, cannot be forgotten. But there's something I can do to move forward. I can tell the truth. I can set the record straight.

Suddenly the images of last May are too much to bear, so vivid that if I close my eyes I'm afraid they'll capture me. That

I'll never escape the memory. But I need to tell someone. Someone needs to know. I've stayed silent, but look where silence has gotten me. Pushing everything away, running, is what has brought us here. I'm ready to stop. Even if we don't come back, at least the truth will.

I touch my thumb to my pocket. I pray. *Please, Claire, hear this. Please, Claire, you need to know.*

I take a deep breath. "You read those articles about Kristen?" I say. "About what happened last May?"

Astor doesn't move, not even to nod, but I press on. I have to tell her.

"I didn't save her," I say. "I couldn't have saved anyone. That was the whole point."

I never thought I'd say this out loud. I thought I'd take this secret to my grave. But now that I've started down the road, I know there is no going back. My words are strong, set, hard—like pieces of clay baked in an oven. They're ready to come out.

I look at Astor. His eyes are unblinking. I imagine I'm talking to Claire when I say, "I went up to the roof that night because I didn't want to live anymore. I went up there to jump."

My memory flashes, calls up the imprinted scene in my mind. Me climbing over the railing. It had all just come apart that week, the grief that I had been trying to keep down low.

The things I had been trying to push out into the ground through my feet. I was barely surviving, and then Trevor broke up with me and I felt like I had lost everything. That there was no point in existing anymore. I remembered the police officer's comment: *For the rest of her life, that girl is going to wish she had died instead.*

He was right. But I couldn't take her place. I could only join her.

Jumping was secondary. Like an afterthought. The only thing that mattered was getting up on that roof.

I know it sounds stupid, unbelievable, even, but I didn't think too much about it. I figured if I got up there, on that ledge, what would need to happen would happen. There was a man who jumped from his terrace in Abigail's building fifty years ago. He lived four floors below her penthouse, and he died on the spot. I remember reading about it in a book of news clippings my dad kept in his study. I figured I didn't have to worry about that part. It would get the job done.

Was I going to jump? The honest answer is that I don't know. I'm not sure. What I do know is that the ledge felt like the only place where I might have a shot at peace. It was the only place in the whole city I felt like it might be quiet. That I might escape the cruel memories that attacked my mind daily—every second, every moment. What came after being up there I couldn't quite get to. I just knew that if I was closer to the edge, there'd be more space. From past and present. From the things I had done and hadn't done. On that ledge there wasn't room for anything else, not memories and not regrets. There wasn't room for anything but this one thing, this one act of over and out. This space—the middle between living and dying.

Kristen just showed up. I was standing on the edge, looking down, watching the cars swaying beneath me, when I heard her behind me.

"Mcalister. Don't." That's what she said.

I turned around, just enough to tell her to go away. "You don't have to be here," I said.

"Please give me your hand." She acted like she hadn't even heard me.

I remember she seemed tall on that roof. Strong. Not the small midwestern girl who sat in the back of English class. She was a warrior up there. She might have been a hero.

"Give me your hand."

I didn't move. I wasn't sure how. When you have that much adrenaline pumping through your body, it's hard to make it do anything. The connection between your brain and limbs loosens—there isn't the same call and response. There wasn't space to feel anything up there, not even fear. I don't think I was sure, if I jumped, whether I'd fall or fly.

Kristen climbed over then. She just stepped up to the wall and dropped one leg over, then the other. In hindsight she should have kept one foot planted on the other side; she should have straddled the stone railing. But I think her body was doing the same thing mine was. It was reacting. She was fearless.

She climbed all the way over so we were both standing on the ledge. No more than sixteen inches wide. Foot. Foot. Foot. Foot.

She took my hand. I let her.

"Just step over with me," she said. She touched my leg like she wanted it to follow her. "You're going to be okay," she said. It wasn't the first time she said it.

"One, two, three." She made a move to lift her foot, and so did I, and they knocked each other. Just a tap, but the shift in balance made her step sideways. Except there was no sideways. There was only sixteen inches and then air.

Our hands were still locked, and I felt her body drop, the snap of contact through our palms, and then my body following, catapulting forward. Down.

I reached around and grabbed the wall. Held on for dear life. She screamed. People came running.

"You're going to be okay," I said. The same words, slipped, mirrored. I don't know whether they were out loud or not. But I know she heard them. I'm sure of it.

I've never used that much strength. I pulled like I was pulling her out from quicksand. Or water. Like I was dragging her out from the bottom of a pool.

I blink and look at Astor. He's watching me with a quiet fascination, like he's sorting through my words. Organizing and categorizing them.

"'The mark of the immature man is that he wants to die nobly for a cause, while the mark of the mature man is that he wants to live humbly for one,'" Astor says.

It's a line from *The Catcher in the Rye*. I just look at him. It's like I'm seeing him for the first time. The real him. The boy who never got over the loss of his mother. Who holds her memory embalmed, like a stuffed deer head on the wall.

And suddenly the thing that binds us, that holds us together, breaks like a rope that splits at the seam.

"Grief isn't a cause, Astor."

Once I say it, the fear begins to evaporate. The fear I've been holding since that day, here, in January. The fear I've had coming out here—what he'll do. Because for the first time tonight I realize that what he's capable of doesn't matter. What matters is me—what *I* can do.

"We're the same," Astor says.

"No," I say, "we're not. We're nothing alike. You haven't let go."

He leans forward. "And you have?"

I look at him. Hard. "I'm about to."

He stops for a split second—poised, hovering—and then: "This will help."

In the next moment, three things happen.

The first is that Astor takes his lighter and holds it out in front of him. Like an offering. Like a candle on an altar. I know what he's going to do before he does it, but I'm not quick enough to stop him.

The second is that I hear voices shouting my name from outside. Voices I recognize. Voices that sound like home.

The third is that Astor takes the shoe out of my hands, drops it into the box, and sets the lighter flame to the edge of the cardboard.

I just sit there for a moment, watching him. So this is it. This is the inherent bad that was always going to come of tonight. I knew we might not make it back. I knew tragedy might strike again here, but I didn't know what form it would take.

Fire.

And then the box explodes. It goes up like a bomb, catapulting us back, away from each other. There is no more time for thought. I cover my face with my hands.

Astor shouts from the other side. There are pieces of

cardboard everywhere, and they're catching the carpet—a meteor shower of fire. I know what has done it. The nail-polish remover. I remember learning about it in some home safety course we had to take at school. The most flammable everyday substances. It was number two.

I quickly scan my brain to see if I have any information stored there that might help me figure out where there is a fire extinguisher. But I come up empty. And the fire is moving faster than the answers.

As the pieces of box catch the carpet, they ignite. They go from embers to full-on flames in no more than a moment. Astor and I are now on opposite sides of a wall of fire. Did he want this? Did he know that that one little lighter would make this big of an impact?

It's then that I jump to my feet.

You think true moments of terror, real instants of adrenaline, only come a few times over the course of one's lifetime. But this is the third this year. Life doesn't deal everyone an even hand; it's just not how it works. My brain knows the drill. It's like my nervous system has shut down. It's too overloaded. By what I've just confessed. By the reality of these flames that continue to lick higher.

But something is different this time too. That panic that's crowded me, that's sat on my chest like a trash compressor and squeezed, is lessening. Even standing here in this split second, calling to Astor, I don't feel afraid. I know something now that I didn't before. I know that my life doesn't have to be about what happened. What I failed to do.

It can be about what I will.

"This way!" I bellow to Astor. I wave my arms above my head and gesture for him to follow me. There is a slice of open air between the fire and doorway that he could slip through, but it's closing quickly. He has to act now. The flames are growing, climbing higher and higher, like some crazed animal that has just been set free. They catch the curtains, transform them into smokestacks. They scramble like they've been waiting a long time to be released.

But Astor doesn't move. He's frozen. And the look in his eyes is one I recognize immediately. It's the same one that stared back at me in the mirror for almost a year. He doesn't know what to do. He doesn't know how to move. He hasn't figured out how to save himself.

"Astor, *now*!"

Fire is loud. It wails and screeches and howls. It cracks things, breaks them into pieces. Drowns out noise. Voices.

But I know he can hear me. I can tell by the way he isn't trying to understand me. He's just not moving.

"Astor!" I scream it again.

The flames lighten, for just a moment, like the exhale of

the tide before a massive wave, and I know it's over. It hits me like the moment I realized that was Hayley at the bottom of the pool. But this time there is no windfall of recognition. No moment of pause.

When I finally managed to haul Kristen back up, when we were both safely on the other side of the railing, out of breath, heaving, hands on knees, I knew I would never try again. I was scared of myself after that, afraid of what I had done. I didn't want to think about it or remember it. The flip side of human beings is terrifying. What we are capable of doing to each other, to ourselves, in any given moment. I didn't know what was down deeper, what would have happened if Kristen hadn't shown up. The endless question, the one I could never answer: Would I have jumped?

But I'm not afraid anymore. And I know, looking at Astor, that he is. Death might have drawn us together, but it's also what has broken us apart.

And in that moment of fear (freezing), life sweeps in.

"Astor!" I make one final attempt to call him, and then I just duck forward, toward him. I dart through the space of air by the wall, but it's not big enough, and I feel the fire bite into my leg. I squeeze my eyes shut against the pain and stick my arm out. I find Astor's shirt underneath my fingertips and I pull. Hard. The adrenaline is back, my old friend, and it helps me get Astor underneath my grip. I turn back around, pushing him in front of me, through, but the space is no longer there. It's closed, sealing us into the back part of Hayley's room. Wall on one side, fire on the other. And it's moving closer.

The heat is unbearable. It's thick and heavy. I shove Astor back against the wall, but there is no relief. The room is being sucked of oxygen. You can hear it being slurped up like soda, then swallowed until there is nothing left.

I look at Astor. He's fading. His eyes are slipping closed. He's already succumbing.

Something about seeing him pressed against the wall, eyes at half-mast, makes me shoot alert. I pull whatever last reserve of will I have. I've never been more determined to live.

I glance over at the windows. The curtains are gone, so are the pink valances, but there are windows, to the side, that don't have any drapery. Hayley insisted on keeping them clean so that it didn't "make it look like a little girl's room." It was like she thought she wore a disguise most of the time. That when she went out in public she was secretly a middle-aged woman. Not a ten-year-old with soft ringlets and baby rose cheeks.

She didn't want screens on the windows either. She liked to look outside and not have it interrupted by some kind of a grid, she said. It was a fight, but she won. My mom had the screens taken off. I remember that now. And these windows don't slide up—they open out.

I grab Astor's hand and run over to the window closest to us. It gives easily, and I feel a rush of sweet, delicious air. Freedom.

I push it out farther and haul Astor up. It's an easy jump to the ground from here. Maybe fifteen feet, no more.

I just need to get him out this window.

"Out," I say.

He doesn't move. He just shakes his head.

"Astor, out!" I'm not sure if I'm talking. My voice is hoarse. Barren. Used up. But how many things could I be saying right now? He knows. He's just not doing it.

And then I realize it. As certain as I saw it behind that fire curtain. As certain as I was when I called Claire and told her the truth: He doesn't want to be saved.

He's happy here, in this fire.

But I won't let someone else die on my watch. I can't. Because for the first time since last January, I want to save myself. I need to. And that means saving him, too.

I close my eyes and then I hoist Astor up by the back and catapult him through the window. I shouldn't be able to lift and maneuver him, but that's the power of compressed moments. They make you able do things that would never be possible in ordinary ones.

Then I'm on the windowsill. I can feel the fire at my back. It could be on me, that's how close it feels. I look down at the grass below, at Astor's body on the ground, unmoving. This time I don't hesitate.

I jump.

CHAPTER SIXTEEN

The grass is so cool on my back that for a second I think maybe I died. This is what heaven would feel like after a fire—cool, wet grass. But then the throbbing in my leg starts in, and I hear Astor moan beside me, and I know I'm still here.

I open my eyes.

Our house is on fire.

It's almost as if it waited for me to leave the building, because in the last—what? Thirty seconds? Minute?—it has taken over. It races through the rooms like a conquering army taking what it has just won.

My parents' bedroom. The study. My old room. Kitchen. Living room.

I always saw my memory as something to run from. It

reminded me of things I didn't want to remember. It kept the past in too sharp detail. It didn't let time do its natural thing—let things yellow, rust, fade. But watching the flames envelop this house—Hayley's grave—I know I've been wrong. Because the memories I've been calling up have been the final ones, but they're not the only ones that are there.

You remember the last moment. They way she looked at the bottom of that pool, what you could have done, what you didn't say. The last fight you had. The fact that I didn't help her inside with her suitcase. But a person, even a house, as it stands burning, is not a moment. It's a lifetime. Hayley was a lifetime. I held her in my arms when she was born. I taught her how to ride a bike and catch fireflies in jars. We baked cookies together. She fell asleep on my chest. She wasn't the girl I was annoyed at in the car on the way to the beach that day. She was my sister. She was everything.

"Caggie!" "Caggie!" The same voices I heard from inside Hayley's room minutes ago come through strong now. Close.

Then Claire is there and Peter, too. I can barely see through the smoke, and they try to drag me away, to move me back. The air is thick, heavy and dense. I'm choking on it. It comes in and fills my lungs like water, and I wonder, briefly, if you can drown in dust.

"Take her to the beach!" Peter shouts at Claire.

Claire puts her arm around me and starts walking me

away, down the path that leads from our house to the shore.

"Astor," I say, but it's more of a cough than anything else.

"It's okay," Claire says gently. "Peter." I can feel her clutching me. Her voice is calm, but her body is tense. A ceiling beam falls a few meters from us, and she slings her arm over me. "Come on," she says firmly.

Instantly Astor and Peter disappear like a magician into his trick. Poof. Gone.

Claire keeps tugging me farther away, toward the beach. She loops her arm under mine and hoists me up by the waist. My burned leg is searing, and I hazard a glance down. My skirt looks like it has melted against my legs, and I can see blood oozing into the plaid. I focus on Claire.

"You're okay," she keeps saying.

I can feel her pulling me tightly to her side. We're off the trail, and the weeds bite at my legs like dogs. We push forward until we reach the sand. I sink my feet down into it. It's cool and dry, and for a moment that's all that matters.

The sky is clear here, and I can see the cloud of smoke—it hovers what seems like just inches from us, like if I reached out I could grab ahold of it. Tug it closer or push it away.

I turn my attention to Claire. She's looking at me like she's trying to figure out whether I'm really there. She keeps touching my arm, and when I turn to her, she throws both arms around me. "Jesus," she says into my shoulder. She's crying.

"Hey," I whisper. "I'm okay." The words make me cough, and I feel Claire's hand on my back.

She hugs me tighter. Sniffs in. "Caggie," she keeps saying.

I lean my head on her shoulder, feel her long, lanky arms around me. I fold my weight into her.

"I'm so sorry," she whispers fiercely.

We break apart and she puts her hands on both of my cheeks. I can see the tears streaming down her face, making clear lines through the dust that's settled there.

"Claire Bear," I say.

She wipes the back of her hand across her face and cranes over me for just a moment. Her eyes are nervous, and then guilty as they look back at me. She's worried about Peter.

"He'll be okay," I say. My voice comes out clear. For a second I have an image of Peter running into the house, trying to save—what?—but I shake my head, force the thought to leave. He's just helping Astor to safety. There isn't anything left in the house to rescue.

And that's when I remember it. The phone in my pocket.

"You came," I say.

Claire looks at me, her eyes big and round and wet. "We were already on our way," she says. "Trevor called after he ran into you, and he said he was worried. Peter and I came to your house. He checked the flower pot on the stoop. I don't know why, but he did. And he saw the key was gone." She stops, coughs, then shakes her head. "I'm so sorry about that article. I know you were pissed at me, but I didn't even know that woman was going to write a story. She was over interviewing my dad. I was just talking. I should have known better. I was just so worried about you. I—"

"Stop," I say. The article feels continents from here. Decades away. "It doesn't matter anymore." But I have to ask her something else, something that I hope she already knows.

"I heard," she says, before I can call up the question. Her eyes are steady, calm. She doesn't even blink. "I listened the whole time."

I hold her gaze for a moment, and the last year passes between us. A million *I'm sorrys* and *pleases* and *I could haves* boiled down into just this—the truth.

"Caggie," she says, rushing forward, all at once. She's talking so quickly it's like her words are jostling one another, trying to get the front spot. "I'm sorry I wasn't there for you. I should have been more. I thought you were doing better, and—"

"It wasn't your fault," I say. "It had nothing to do with you."

She shakes her head. Fresh tears sprout. "I thought I could get you to move on."

I put my hand on her shoulder and pull her toward me. Even with the smoke and ash I can smell her perfume in the air—faint, light, but still holding on. "You did," I say.

I was wrong about lying. It's not easy; it's hard. It weighs on you—every single untruth. They build and grow, like weeds in a garden. They take over. They knot things down and snuff them out. Just one can ruin a field of flowers.

"I love you," she says fiercely. "I would have done anything to protect you. I'd—"

But before she can finish, she gives a little yelp. Her arms slacken, and I see Peter. He's coming down toward us, and he has Astor slung over his arm. At first glance it's hard to tell whether Astor is dead or alive, he's leaning so heavily on Peter. But then I see his head lob to the side and lift back, and I know he's in there somewhere.

Claire runs over to them. I limp behind. I hook Astor around the waist and set him down in the sand. Peter is breathing so hard he can't talk, and Claire throws her arms around him. He holds her close, presses his nose into the crook of her neck.

It should be strange, seeing my brother and my best friend like this, but nothing is strange anymore. Or everything is. Beside me Astor is rocking slowly, his head in his hands.

I know it's over. That his father is right: He needs help. I lean down and place a hand on his back, palm flat. He looks up at me, and in the instant our eyes lock, I know he knows too.

You can't share grief. In the end, when the building burns, you're still left with your own pieces. Your own shattered picture frames. You have to pick up what is yours—choose to carry it, bury it, or say good-bye.

"I'm sorry," Astor says. Muffled. Dim. But I hear him.

"Me too," I say.

Not one of us talks after that. We just sit and watch in silence. Even later, once the fire trucks arrive and there is nothing left but black beams, coals, and dirt, we don't say anything. We don't have to. We're each busy deciding what we'll take from there and what we'll leave behind.

CHAPTER SEVENTEEN

I'd like to say that Astor got help, that he came to me and apologized for what had happened, explained how he now understood the error of his ways. That he was learning to let go of his mother, move on to a clear future, and carry her brightest memory like a star in his pocket. But that didn't happen.

We called our parents after the fire died down, but they, too, were already on their way. They had been alerted by the security system in the house. The fire department called when they saw the first flames. My dad showed up with my mom. I guess he was around. Maybe he'd never left. He got to me first, pulled me into a hug so tight it lifted me off the ground.

He started crying. My father. My buttoned-up, hedge-fund

father. I had never seen him cry before. He hadn't even cried at Hayley's funeral. But when they got there and he saw me, he started. He bent down next to me. He took me into his arms. "I'm so sorry," he said. "I promise it will be better now. We'll get your leg fixed up. We'll take care of this. It's all going to be okay."

He still cared. His concern over Astor was because he wanted me to be safe. I realized it was true: No matter what had happened, I had never stopped being his daughter.

"I'm sorry," I said to him. And then it just came out. I couldn't stop it. "I'm sorry I didn't save her."

My dad held me close. I could feel his tears on my face. "Not your fault," he said. I wasn't sure he meant it until I pulled back and looked at him. I saw his face. It reminded me so much of mine. He didn't even have to say what he did next: "It was mine."

We were all carrying her loss. We were all carrying the guilt of losing her. I knew, in that moment, my father's arms around me, that Hayley would never come back—but I also knew, for the first time since she died, that I wasn't alone. Not anymore. I was part of a family. *My* family.

Astor moved immediately after the fire. It might have been to London; it might have been to Africa; it might have been to a facility upstate. I have no idea. His father told him he wasn't allowed to see me again, and sure enough, the last time I ever saw him was behind the glass of his father's town car pulling out of the fire station. I e-mailed, once, to ask him whether he was okay, but I never got a response.

That's real life. Things don't always work out the way you think they will. They're not so neat and tidy. But people come into your life with a purpose—I see that now. Claire likes to say that people cross your path for a reason, a season, or a lifetime. Astor was a reason. Hayley, though? Hayley is a lifetime. I know now that to let go of her, I don't have to forget her.

"Are you almost done?" The voice snaps me back to the present moment.

I shake my head. "Impatient much? You were the one who wanted me to write this article."

"Yeah, I know," he says. "But I'd like to get out of here before sunup."

Trevor and I are in the offices of the *Journal*. We're working late—the magazine has to go to Mrs. Lancaster for approval tomorrow (she's already extended our deadline), and in it is going to be a story. My story.

"Big plans?" I ask, running the cursor over a line.

"I need to work on Tuesday," he says.

I turn to face him, and Trevor smiles. He's got this

wonderful smile, the kind that feels like it's plugged in somewhere—like one thousand volts of light.

"I'm out of here." Trevor and I both look up as Kristen stands from her desk and slings her bag over her shoulder. "If you want me to proofread that, then you have to send it by midnight, got it?" She points to my computer screen and raises her eyebrows.

I turn to Trevor. "Someone is getting kind of bossy."

Trevor shrugs. "Sometimes you need tough love, Caggs."

Kristen smiles and gives us a little wave, and I watch as the door shuts behind her. We're becoming friends, slowly. Mostly at the *Journal*. She's very different than I thought she was—not at all the shy, insecure girl I always wrote her off to be. We talk honestly now. It started with my telling her the thing I should have said a long time ago, the thing that I could never bring myself to, not until now: *Thank you.*

I lean back from the computer and stretch. "If I don't finish writing this tonight, it's not going to have a shot at being included."

Trevor nods. "Okay," he says. He brings his chair closer to mine, so they're right up against each other. "How can I help?"

We work for another hour. Trevor formats the issue, and I finish my article. It feels nice up here with him, a new kind of normal. The panic still crops up sometimes, the pain, but

REBECCA SERLE

there is a calm that comes with having seen the worst and weathered the storm.

Trevor and I are going on our first official date on Tuesday. Well, our first second official date. We're taking it slow this time. Things are different now, but I'm learning that maybe that's okay.

After the fire I kept trying to figure out if I could ever get back to where I was with Trevor before, if we could have the kind of relationship we had when Hayley was still alive. What I didn't realize, and what I'm still learning, is that we don't need to get back anywhere. We just need to move forward.

It feels good to finally tell my own side of the story, and to be honest. I'm setting the record straight about Kristen. It's time to speak up. It's not fair for her to take the fall anymore. It never was. When I asked her why she lied for me, why she didn't just correct people, she told me this: "You needed the secret kept for you more than I needed the truth to come out."

When I finish the piece, I give it to Trevor. "Hand it over," he says. "It's going to print."

"Do you think Mrs. Lancaster will even okay it?" I ask. "I haven't exactly been a model representative."

"I'm pretty sure we can work something out." He smiles at me, and exaggerates a kissing motion with his lips.

"Are you saying you're willing to fulfill Mrs. Lancaster's fantasies to get her to publish this?"

Trevor picks up my hand from the keyboard. His eyes search mine, and when they find me, I feel myself melt into him. It's warm here. Home. "Caggie," he says. "I'd do anything for you."

I should probably say, for the record, that Abigail Adams and I are no longer friends. When I got back to school, after the fire, she didn't seem so interested anymore. "You burned Astor," she said. I couldn't tell whether she was mad about him not coming back or about not being the one to break the news about what happened at the beach. "We were friends—you should have told me something was wrong." But either way, in the next breath she declared, "I've had enough of your drama for one lifetime," and sauntered off with Constance and Samantha at her heels.

It goes without saying that Trevor and I haven't been invited to her end-of-the-year party in May. Neither has Kristen, for that matter. I think the three of us are going to go see a movie instead. Something funny. I agree with Abbey: I've had enough drama too.

Did I ever mention that our Hamptons house was my grandfather's? Well, it was, and when Peter cleaned it out, he kept everything. Three generations' worth of stuff. He put it all in a storage unit in New Jersey, across the bridge, and the next morning, after the *Journal*, we go to unload it.

I'm sitting in the town car between my mom and dad. Peter is up front with the driver. Mom has been chatting the whole way over. This running commentary about the scenery, how nice the weather is. "Do you think we should go back into the city or find somewhere around here to eat after? Or we could go home. We could make breakfast at night! Remember when we used to do that?" She keeps rambling, about whether or not we have pancake mix, when my dad reaches over and takes her hand. My mom moves her fingers between his, and they hold them that way, resting in my lap, until we get to the warehouse.

Peter runs out to get the keys, and the three of us get out of the car. We follow him back, to the farthest unit on the left.

"You think we could order Serafina from here?" Dad asks, and Mom starts laughing. It's the first time I've heard her laugh in months, maybe even a year. The sound rolls off the metal storage units like water on a tin roof—loud, too close, and yet somehow comforting. Dad smiles too. He's here now, really here. I look over at my parents, both dressed in jeans and sweaters. Dad rolls his sleeves up and takes the key from Peter. He cranks the door open.

We stand in a row as we look at all the boxes. No one talks

for a moment, and then Dad says: "You did a great job, P." He puts a hand on Peter's back and an arm around me.

"Let's get started," Mom says.

Let me tell you something—change is seeing my formerly Chanel-clad mother decked out in jeans, being the first one to make her way through a dusty storage unit.

Mom steps in and pulls the string of the overhead swing light, and then we all fall in line behind.

Dad and Peter head to the back, and Mom and I stay up front. We sit down on some boxes. "Just start opening," Dad calls. "There is no right way to do this."

Mom opens a box and I suck in my breath. It's full of paintings. Hayley's paintings. Mom unrolls one, and I see her hand fly to her mouth. It's unfinished, but it looks like it was going to be a bird. Hayley's signature. Mom covers her face with her hands.

I go over to her and wrap my arms around her. We stay that way for a long time, my head on her shoulder, the piece of canvas pressed between us.

"I am lucky to have you," she says finally. She wipes the back of her hand over her eyes. She doesn't say *I'm sorry,* or *My mascara must be a mess,* or anything else. Just "I'm lucky to have you." And for the first time, I think maybe she means it, maybe she doesn't think that Hayley would still be here if it wasn't for me. Maybe we're all—me, Dad, Peter, and Mom—finally starting to see what we have left.

We stay in that unit for nine hours, sorting boxes, laughing over some memories, crying over others. Claire stops by around lunchtime to bring us sandwiches—and to see Peter. They're well past Claire's six-week period at this point, and I'm getting used to it. They both seem happy, and although Peter is back at USC, he's still in a lot of weekends, and she goes to visit him, too. "I may be a California girl after all," she said to me when she came back last time.

They make out for a few minutes behind some boxes where they think no one can see, but she doesn't stay long. She knows this is a family moment, and I'm grateful to her for that. That's one thing about Claire: Where it really counts, like in a dark storage unit, or on a one-sided cell phone call, she gets it.

"Here whenever you need me," she says on her way out. She squeezes my arm, tucks her chin on my shoulder.

"I know," I say.

I take one thing from today. It's a photograph of Hayley I snapped when she was eight. I'm not exactly the world's best photographer, but I was always really proud of this picture. She's on a bike in it, and she's balancing with her hands, her feet off the ground. She looks a little like she's flying, a bird ready to take flight.

She's not looking at me, exactly, more like behind me,

and she's squinting, the sun in her eyes. I took the picture with an ancient camera, the kind that has real film, and I remember struggling to find somewhere that would develop it, that didn't just use digital. But this is New York. You can find anything here. I had it blown up and framed, and I gave it to Hayley on her ninth birthday. She liked it, but she didn't really think too much of it at the time. There was something about it, though. Something that always drew me back. The way she was looking behind me, squinting. The way her arm was reaching out. It was like she saw something I didn't.

There are moments, if I look back, that lead up to her death. Moments that could have foreshadowed what happened. That we were always going to end up there. That every decision, every choice, was going to get us out to the house, her to that pool. Does that still make it my fault? I'm not sure. Ten percent of the time I think maybe it was just an accident. That what happened to Hayley wasn't because of anything I did or didn't do. It was just what happened. But that's only ten percent. The other ninety still misses her, still blames myself. But six months ago there was no ten percent, so maybe it grows. Maybe, over time, you get to fifty-fifty.

I see Peter tossing a football up to my dad, my mom sorting through linens to the right of me, and I think, I *know*, that I'm learning—that we all are. We are redefining what our story is. We are the Caulfields. We are a family. And it doesn't matter anymore what other people think. I understand, now, that your own identity, your past, has nothing to do with the way others see you. Being a hero isn't about someone else's definition. Not Abigail's and not Constance's. Not the *Post*'s. Not even Claire's. Being a hero is about one thing: the way you see yourself.

So, okay, we've come to the end. But the truth is that stories revise themselves. There is another one here. A different version. And when I tell it now, I tell that one. It's changed, as I have. People don't like to say that the space between lies and truth is very, very small. It's there, but it's just a whisper away. One foot over a ledge. A lit match before contact. A line in a dust-covered book. A bird about to take flight. At a certain point, you have to decide the truth for yourself.

Now when I begin, it goes like this: Most great works of literature have a hero at their core. This story is no exception.

Acknowledgments

A very special thanks . . .

To Hannah Brown Gordon, my dearest friend. When I write, it is still always to you.

To Mollie Glick, my incredible agent, who continues to be a fierce advocate for my career, and more importantly, for me. You have flown this plane through every storm, and you have never let us down.

To Liesa Abrams, my editor, whose direction and vision have made this book something to be proud of. I am eternally grateful.

To Leila Sales, my writing partner, my wacky buddy

cop, my plus one, my Sophia Grace—you give me confidence. I never want to do this alone. I'm so lucky I don't have to.

To Lexa Hillyer, my plot (life) goddess. We are awesome. Now let's go talk more about it.

To Anica Rissi, who will always be editor of mine.

To Michael Strother, a keen editor and a man of excellent television taste. Cupcake Andy, I adore you.

To Paul Crichton, Janet Ringwood, and Lydia Davis, who support my wacky ideas, find new ones, and make the fun part, well, fun.

To everyone at Pulse and Foundry for providing the most rocking (and stylish) literary homes a girl could ask for.

To Kathleen Hamlin for helping me with anything and everything and doing it all with a smile.

To Brad and Yfat Gendell, who continue to champion Rebecca Serle in every form. What can I say? When I am seated at your dinner table, a kid on my lap, I am home.

To my beautiful, sensitive, loving parents who have never passed up an opportunity to express their pride. Thank you for seeing me just as I am, and for letting me know that was perfect, and enough.

To the city of New York that has sometimes kicked me

down, but never kicked me out—It has always been worth it.

Finally to the wonderful readers, bloggers, librarians and teens who have supported *When You Were Mine*.

Thank you, thank you.

RIVETED

BY *simon* teen ♥

BELIEVE IN YOUR SHELF

Visit RivetedLit.com & connect with us on social to:

DISCOVER NEW YA READS

READ BOOKS FOR FREE

DISCUSS YOUR FAVORITES

SHARE YOUR IDEAS

ENTER SWEEPSTAKES FOR THE CHANCE TO WIN BOOKS

Follow @SimonTeen on

to stay up to date with all things Riveted!

Leap into summer with these

swoon-worthy

reads by *New York Times*
bestselling author Morgan Matson.

This is what happens after happily ever after.

The companion series to the *New York Times* bestselling

MARA DYER TRILOGY

An unforgettable novel about the ghosts of the past, the power of connection, and the bonds of sisterhood. . . .